THE DIVIDED HEART

The Strong Family Saga
Book Three

Ros Rendle

SAPERE
BOOKS

THE DIVIDED HEART

Published by Sapere Books.

20 Windermere Drive, Leeds, England, LS17 7UZ,
United Kingdom

saperebooks.com

ISBN: 978-1-80055-543-3

ACKNOWLEDGEMENTS

Sapere Books have a very talented team of editors and publicists. This book is all the better for their perceptive care. They also engender a great friendship ethic between their authors. I'm truly lucky to be part of that family, so it's with huge thanks to them for the success of this series and others of my books.

CHAPTER 1

Yorkshire, 1975

Heather Rawson's final task on her second day at The Beeches Care Home for the Elderly was to call in on Iris Strong before she left. She was a new resident, and the staff wanted to make sure she was okay.

"Evening and night staff will help her change. They make sure all the residents are settled for bed," the matron informed her. "Oh, and she likes to be called Izzy."

Heather followed the directions to Izzy's room. The door was ajar. She knocked gently but there was no response, so she pushed it open and peeped round. The old lady was sitting in a chair on the other side of the room, but she made no sound.

What if she's snuffed it? Heather thought. She withdrew her head and grimaced. *Not a very sympathetic way to put it, I suppose. Can't have that attitude if I'm going to work here. I'll have to get used to it.* She took a deep breath and crept in.

Izzy was wrapped in a lilac woollen scarf and slumped in a wingback chair near the window. Heather saw from her silhouette against the still-bright afternoon that her chin had sunk down and wisps of fine hair had escaped from her bun. Heather tip-toed slowly across the room. As she neared, she noticed the slight rise and fall of Izzy's chest. Heather felt her shoulders relax. The old soul was in a deep sleep. She turned to leave her in peace.

"No, NO!"

Heather gasped, and her heart leapt. She turned back to Izzy, who appeared to be fighting something off with her hands, wiping and clawing at her body as she slept. Her head rolled from one side to the other.

Panic surged through Heather. Then she thought, *I'm sure I've read somewhere that you shouldn't wake a person in the middle of a nightmare.*

Izzy continued to pick and scrabble at her jumper and skirt.

Was it an insect swarm she saw in her dream? Was it some grimy, syrupy substance that stuck to her? Heather watched, mesmerized by Izzy's horror as she writhed and mumbled, "No, no!" Then, more loudly, "Mind, the wire … cut you… You … reach, reach higher. NO!" The old lady was now gasping. She moaned in despair.

I can't allow this to continue, Heather told herself. *It's appalling.* She bent down beside Izzy and put her cool hand to her forehead, calmly stroking her hair. "Shh, there, there," she whispered.

Slowly the anguish subsided, and Heather removed her hand. Izzy shifted in her chair and awoke. She looked around, dazed. After several moments, she seemed to recall where she was. "Oh, hello." Izzy's eyes gradually focused.

"I think you were having a bad dream," Heather prompted.

"Oh dear, did I disturb someone?"

"No, not at all. I was a little worried for you, though."

"I do seem to have the same dream quite often these days, but no matter." Izzy flapped her hand. "It's just a dream. It all started a long, long time ago; before you were born and even before your parents were born, I imagine."

"Would it help to tell me about it? I don't wish to pry, but sometimes if things are shared…" Heather's words fizzled out.

"It's a long story, and I suppose it started when I was little more than a child myself. That's how it seems now, looking back. I was only twenty-four or five. Old, I suppose, to be finishing my wider education, so to speak, but the war changed everything." She shrugged. "I think you'd soon be bored."

"Oh no, not at all. Let me fetch us a cup of Ovaltine. It will be comforting, and you can tell me."

Despite her assurances, Heather dithered. Then she made her choice. If she was to turn over a new leaf, make a success of this job, then this might be the start. To brook no further argument with either Izzy or herself, she hurried along towards the lift that would take her down to the little kitchen. A man was waiting at the lift door. She'd seen him yesterday, her first day of working here. Now she guessed he was a cleaner from his tin bucket, cylinder of Vim, Mr Sheen, and bottle of Mop & Glo.

"I've pressed the button." He spoke with the local Yorkshire accent.

As they rode down to the ground floor, Heather was embarrassed and unnaturally tongue-tied. She'd often been accused of being frightened of silence and covering that with chatter. With his blond hair and impish smile, this bloke reminded her of her bastard ex, Kev, who she was desperate to erase from her memory.

In the confined space, she tried to look anywhere but at him, but she couldn't resist a peek. Okay, this bloke was tall and handsome; slim but broad-shouldered. Heather could see a triangle of tanned chest at the neck of his T-shirt, like someone from the romance novels her mother took to her lonely bed every night. His hair sat just below his collar, but it was his eyes that really caught her attention. They were light green and piercing. She shuddered.

Was he smirking at her? Arrogant sod. She looked away.

"You finished your shift, then? You're new here, aren't you? My name's Will, by the way," he persisted.

"No, I'm going to find the kitchen to make a cup of Ovaltine for Izzy Strong." Heather wasn't going to share her name with him. No way. He could find it out by some other means.

"Down there," he said and jerked his head as, thankfully, the lift doors opened.

"Yes, I know." Heather hadn't been certain of the way, but she turned defiantly and trotted along the corridor. The thick carpet deadened all sound. On one wall hung a print of a beautiful woman wearing a dress with a vibrant yellow collar, her face painted in shades of blue and green. There was another print that was reminiscent of Kandinsky's style but diverged from his usual colour palette; the artist had used tones of orange, brown, black and olive green. The two pictures added vibrancy to an otherwise plain hallway.

White-painted doors, some of which were open, lined the other side of the corridor. Surreptitiously Heather glanced into one or two of the rooms. They reminded her of a posh hotel, but personal belongings sat upon the chests of drawers, and photographs of the residents' family members hung on some walls. She'd never worked anywhere like this before. It was a far cry from the office. Still, beggars couldn't be choosers and she needed the work.

Once in the kitchen, Heather found the milk in the new-looking fridge and a pan in the cupboard. Her mind turned back to the good-looking bloke in the lift as she made the hot drinks. She huffed, deciding she did not like him, not one little bit. *He might be gorgeous, but he's not my type at all, not anymore*, she thought.

Back upstairs and with two steaming mugs of Ovaltine, Heather pulled up a wooden chair from beside the bed and sat next to Izzy. "I'm new here. My name's Heather Rawson." She searched her brain for something to say to get the story rolling.

"I'm twenty-five. Isn't that about the age you said you were when your story began?"

"It started a long, long time before the wall and the wire. It was in Berlin, and it was 1927. That's when I first met Garrit." Izzy paused and sipped her drink. She gazed out of the window, and a small smile played at the corners of her soft, purple-tinged lips.

Heather took a sip of her drink. Sensing a good story was about to come her way, she settled on her chair, tucking her feet around its legs. "The wire," she prompted and leaned forward.

"I didn't know then how my life would change, or what dangers there might be."

CHAPTER 2

Berlin, 1927

For the past few months, Izzy had been staying at her friend Gisela's family home. The previous evening, there had been talk of going to the cinema to see the wildly expensive expressionist science fiction film that everyone was talking about but in the end it had been more dancing and some drinking.

"I had such a good time last night." Izzy stretched in bed and then curled up under the covers again.

"You and Max Achterberg danced a lot. He looked handsome in his uniform," Gisela said.

"He's such a flirt. He called me his sugar plum child and asked me to call him darling. I said, 'under no circumstances,' and he pretended to sulk, but in such a charming manner. He gave me a squeeze while we danced, and I gave his arm a smack." Izzy tucked up her knees and laughed.

"I counted at least six officers buzzing around the honey pot. And you were flirting outrageously with each, so don't play the innocent now, missy. There are many English girls here in Berlin. You may have stiff competition if you play too hard to get," Gisela said.

"Oh, don't worry about me. I got asked to go to the opera, to see a film, and to go walking, each by a different boy. They all look so divine in their shiny boots and smart uniforms," Izzy said.

"And you were certainly able to enjoy the company you had last night, outrageous minx!"

"If you wished to see outrageous, you should have watched the way my sister Delphi behaved. She was dreadful during the war. I'm sure I only heard the tip of it because I was so much younger, but she ended up having to go abroad," Izzy said.

"Ooh, tell all, do," Gisela urged. "We missed so much during and after the war."

"No! I've told you too much already about our little family skeleton in the closet." Izzy flung back the covers. "I'm getting up. Come on, lazybones. We can't stay here any longer if we are to be presentable before morning coffee. Someone may call, and I don't want to be found like this and miss all the fun."

Izzy was older than some to be extending her education on the continent, but the war had led to so many changes and delays. Her eldest sister Rose and her husband Michael, for example, were only just finding their feet. At last they had moved into a great mausoleum of a hunting lodge in Glossop that the Duke of Norfolk had allowed them, in which they would run their school. As for Delphi, goodness only knew what she was up to in Australia, although having a child might have slowed her down.

As Izzy came running down the stairs, she was grateful for the comfortable cotton day dress, with its hem just below her knees and her low-heeled Oxford shoes. It was so good to be free of the confines of all those undergarments, too. Her figure suited the latest style of dress, with its long bodice and the belt around her hips which accentuated her slight, boyish shape. She'd hated the long skirts of her teenage years.

She brushed the finger waves of her short hair away from her face as she approached the table at the foot of the stairs. She saw the letter lying on the salver. It was addressed to her, and she knew straight away who it was from. The flimsy blue paper and distinctive Australian postmark told her it was Delphi.

Not like her to be writing to me, of all people, she thought as she turned the letter over.

"Who's that from?" Gisela's voice interrupted Izzy's musings.

"It's from my sister." Izzy's forehead creased.

"It was only a couple of days ago that Rose wrote. I wonder why this one is following so quickly."

"It's not from Rose. It's from Delphi. See the postmark?"

"*Ich bin überrascht.* You were only just mentioning her, the black sheep." Gisela nudged Izzy's elbow and raised her eyebrows.

"She and I never got on particularly well. Rose is a darling and always kept the peace, but Delphi…" Izzy picked up the slim knife which lay on the table and ripped the flimsy paper along its two folds. Unfurling it, she began to read.

Dear Izzy,
I hope this finds you 'in the pink'. I don't doubt you will be surprised to receive this.

That's true enough, Izzy thought.

The fact is, I am thinking of travelling back to England for a while. Flora is old enough to make the long journey. She is pestering me to meet her English family and I, too, long to return and make amends. George's mother and father have been like my own and the life here has been a godsend, under the circumstances, but things are changing and now it's time to come home — for a while, at least.

The thing is, Izzy, do you think I will be welcomed? Papa writes regularly, and I sometimes used to hear from Mama occasionally while she was alive. I even get letters from Rose from time to time. But will Rose be happy enough for me to come, after our great falling out before I left all those years ago?

Please write back as soon as you can and put my mind to rest. I am in a real pickle about this, and Flora keeps demanding an answer.

Izzy had always been puzzled about that argument between her sisters. Something to do with Michael, but she never really got to the bottom of it. It was well in the past now, though.

Izzy handed the letter to Gisela who, she saw, was standing and exhibiting her impatience for information by sighing and stomping around.

"I see," said her friend, having skimmed the letter. "Well, I don't really, because I still don't know why she is in Australia, of all places. And who is Flora? Is she her child?" Her eyebrows shot up. "Ah, I think I do see."

"Flora was born near the end of the war … in Australia. I can't go into all that now. Oh, honestly, if she comes home, I suppose I shall be expected to go back too. I don't want to do that. It's too much fun here. How is it she can control everyone, even from the other side of the world? That is so unfair. I have so much more freedom here, and besides, *Oberleutnant* Max Achterberg would miss me." She laughed to cover her resentment. Tucking the letter into her pocket, she danced a circle and headed for the parlour. "Come along, Gisela, I'm starved."

"We better get a move on. Breakfast will be finished by now, but we may be able to persuade Addie to bring us coffee and something light."

"I love your German habit of *pausenbrot*. It's very civilised to have a bite between meals. It stops us eating a vast amount at dinner."

"Especially when we have a fencing lesson this afternoon. We'd be rolling around the floor," Gisela said.

"Oh yes, goody. Herr Schmidt is so sweet and not a bit like an instructor would be in England. Did you see? He stands behind me and takes my arms to place them correctly. I swear I felt his breath on my cheek and nearly swooned."

"Honestly, Izzy, you have such imagination!"

They entered the little parlour and rang for the long-suffering Addie to leave her kitchen and bring their snack. "I'm so pleased that your Papa managed to arrange this with my parents," Gisela said, taking Izzy's hand and dancing around to face her before they sat. "We could all have lost touch for good during the war."

"It's fortunate I kept in touch with Frau Schröder. If she hadn't got to Switzerland when the war broke out, that would have been that. She's been a brick in helping to set it all up."

"Fortunate that she kept in touch with us too. *Mumie* was very relieved that she made it over the border in time. Still, that was ages ago. Lucky, I say, that links between our two countries were so strong and survived all that aggression."

"Yes, family ties have been strong enough," Izzy said. "Your Kaiser and our King were close before all that, and many English people have German friends and relations too."

"Well, anyway, it means we are firm chums again. We'll always be having fun together," Gisela said.

"But tomorrow afternoon we are to go to that lecture on contemporary novelists. That won't be so amusing," Izzy reminded Gisela.

"This week's edition of *Vati* reported that Thomas Mann is coming all the way from Munich, so we're lucky to hear him. He said he may speak of the art colony he's just been to. That might be fun and a little interesting. It depends who else is to attend," Gisela said. "Last time I went to a similar thing, there was a very lively set with several young men, too."

"Oh, well, it might not be so awful then." Izzy giggled.

The lecture was not as boring as Izzy had first imagined, and afterwards the two girls and a group of friends went to the Unter den Linden and sat at the tables outside the Café König.

"Quick, grab those chairs. If we push these tables together, we can sit as a group," one young man said.

There was a lot of shuffling and jostling. With giggling from the girls and lively banter from the boys, they got themselves organised.

Izzy plonked down onto a chair with her knees together but feet splayed. "Phew, that was energetic," she said as she found herself squashed between Gisela and a dark-haired young man with brown eyes that seemed to sparkle with humour. He looked down at her as she slumped, so she sat up and smiled at him.

"What would you like to drink?" he asked.

Coffee started to arrive. It came in tall glass cups set on dainty mats. *Spritzgebaeck* fingers with their rich chocolate ends looked mouth-wateringly light. While awaiting hers, Izzy was conscious of the man at her elbow and steadfastly tried not to keep looking at him. With her head down, she did manage one sideways peep up, only to find he was watching her. Uncharacteristically confused, she gazed across the pavement.

There were crowds passing, with ladies in fashionable hats and gauzy dresses, men in smart suits with briefcases, and sometimes men linking arms with other men.

"Oh, my word, he's wearing make-up." Izzy grabbed Gisela's arm and leaned in to whisper as she nodded in the direction of two men with their arms around each other.

"That's Berlin for you," Gisela said. "It's a lively place, as you're discovering. It's vibrant and easy. That's why all the artists come here. There are certain parts of the city that we probably won't go to, though. Certainly not without a chaperone."

"There are some places that are, shall we say, an education," the young man next to her said. "May I introduce myself? My name is Garrit Shain."

"Garrit Schön? Garrit the beautiful?"

"Not Schön, Shain," Garrit laughed. "But it does mean beautiful. It's Jewish, not German, that's all."

"Well, Garrit the beautiful, pleased to meet you. I'm Iris Strong, but people call me Izzy."

"And are you as strong as I am beautiful?" He asked the question with a wicked twinkle in his eye.

Izzy laughed. *What an attractive fellow he is*, she thought. *I like the dimple in his cheek when he smiles. This afternoon really has improved.*

CHAPTER 3

Yorkshire, 1975

Heather was enchanted. "Berlin sounds like it was a daring and exciting place."

"I suppose it was, but we were young, and I was away from home with all that attention. I was a bit of a novelty to those young men, with my funny accented German. I'd learned it at home in my youth with Frau Schröder, but even though she used to slap her book on the table at me for my pronunciation, I think I still spoke with an English twang. Yes, it was exciting." With that, Izzy gave a yawn.

"I'm sorry. I've kept you talking all this time. It's getting late, and I must write up my diary before I go home. Perhaps you would tell me some more of your story soon."

"I will if you want, but I'm not sure you will find it that interesting. I'm sure you young people have your own excitement."

"Goodnight, Izzy, and thank you. I have a feeling your life has been much more interesting than mine is likely to be."

"Goodnight, my dear."

As Heather was walking to where she had left her bike, she was preoccupied with what she had been told. Her brain was fizzing with curiosity. This was the first time she had heard anything about those times from an older person. Her only surviving grandparent now lived abroad.

She was still deep in thought when someone called her name, and she looked around to see who it was.

Oh no. The last person I want to bump into at this hour, she thought.

"Do you want a lift somewhere?" Will called across the car park as he stood next to a battered little Fiat.

"No," Heather answered. "Thank you," she added, aware that she sounded rude. Although she was happy to deter him, childhood habits drummed into her by her now absent dictatorial father remained.

"Sure? It's no trouble."

"Perfectly sure, thank you. I have my bike." She indicated it propped up against the wall.

Will shrugged, and Heather let out her tension with a breath.

As she cycled home, she couldn't stop thinking of what Izzy had told her. She had little idea of Germany, never mind in the 1920s. She would have to go to the library. There were so many questions to be answered. Why had Izzy been shouting about a wire in her sleep? She hadn't mentioned any wire in her story. Were the Nazis in power that early? What happened with Garrit? He sounded nice. *I wish I could have met him,* thought Heather. *He was dishy, I imagine.* Izzy's parents must have been very forward-thinking to send her to Berlin alone. *My father wouldn't have. He didn't allow me anything like that amount of freedom. Hmm. Sod him anyway.* She could think that now, knowing he wasn't going to show up any time soon, since he was with his floozy in Spain. She could persuade herself she was fine without him, but the tentacles of his dominance had left an indelible mark upon her, no matter how brave she could pretend to be.

As soon as Heather arrived home, she heard the clatter of the kettle on the gas.

"So, how was your day?" Her mother's voice travelled along the hallway before Heather could escape upstairs.

Heather sat down at the kitchen table and poured out Izzy's story. "I had such a fright when she cried out in her sleep."

June Rawson frowned. "She must have a ton of stuff bottled up inside to be like that."

"Can you imagine her mum and dad letting her go to Germany? I think she was going to a family they knew or something like that, but I wouldn't have been allowed to do that, would I?"

"No, love. I couldn't see your Dad letting you do that."

"He never even wanted me to go down the road to the church youth club, did he?"

"We did have a bit of a battle about that, yes."

"A bit!"

"He was only concerned for you."

"You don't have to stick up for him now, Mum. He's long gone, and since we've not heard hide nor hair of him for years... Anyway, the only downside at my new job, so far, anyway, is this bloke. He's a cleaner, or maybe a caretaker. Anyway, I don't like him."

"Oh? He's not the misbehaving sort, is he?"

"No, Mum, nothing like that. He just thinks he's God's gift to women. He's good-looking, but so arrogant. The old folk seem to think he's wonderful, from what I gathered today, but he definitely reminds me of Kevin."

"Oh dear. Steer clear of him, then. Mind you, if you'd stood up to Kev a bit more, he wouldn't have walked all over you and ended up cheating."

"Maybe, but I didn't want to risk losing him ... then."

"Although that's exactly what happened, love."

"Yes, well ... this chap is simply a conceited young oaf," Heather said with feeling.

"Young, is he?"

"Well, my sort of age, I suppose, but so big-headed."

June collected up the empty mugs and turned to the sink. "Mmm," was all she said. Then, "When are you seeing Brian again? Such a steady chap, he is."

"Oh, I don't know. Steady and a bit boring really, Mum. I'm not sure about him."

"Not like Kev, you mean. Maybe he's what you need."

It was Heather's turn to respond with, "Mmm."

Heather bowled along on her bike in the early morning sunshine. Her hair escaped from under her helmet and flew out behind her. She'd had to pull a big elastic band around her wide trouser leg, so it didn't get caught in the chain, but she didn't care if it looked a bit odd. It wasn't far to The Beeches.

The few pedestrians out this early smiled as they saw her. She sang and whistled The Mixtures' 'Pushbike Song'. It had been in the charts five years ago; 1970, when she'd been 'nobbut a lass' as her Dad would have said. She determinedly shut his voice from her mind. The few lyrics of the song she remembered fitted well with the rhythm of her pedals. It must have been on her mum's transistor radio this morning. She'd just started listening to Pennine Radio. It played old-fashioned stuff, but right now it suited her mood and she smiled as she rode.

She parked her bike at the side of the building, sniffing the air as she removed her helmet. It was so fresh, even with the early spring mist. The two ancient copper beech trees on the front lawn seemed to be home to hundreds of birds. Their singing was joyous.

"Morning." Heather greeted Sue at the reception desk and smiled. "I'm to work alongside a lady called Mary in the craft room this morning. Not sure of the way."

"If you'd just like to wait a minute, someone will come to take you up. I can't leave here. Mary's been here for quite a while. She's lovely, you'll like her. She really knows her stuff." Just then, Will walked through the reception area, and the young woman behind the desk caught his attention. "Oh, Will, this is Heather. Would you show her up to the craft room, please?"

"We've met." He grinned at Heather and she shrank inside.

What is it with him? she thought grumpily.

He looked over his shoulder at her as he led the way. She gazed in front and avoided eye contact, following him in determined silence.

"Mary, this is Heather." He addressed a middle-aged lady as they entered a large L-shaped room labelled CRAFT in jazzy capital letters.

"Oh, thanks, Will, you lovely man," Mary said and gave him a wink.

"Go on with you," he answered. "You're nobbut an old flirt."

She nudged his ribs. "Get back to your cupboard then, if you've nothing else for me." Mary smiled at his retreating backside. "He's such a lovely boy. He's the caretaker and he's so kind-hearted, he'll do anything for anyone. They all love him here," she added.

Mmm, not me, Heather thought, but she smiled politely.

The room was in the same style as the rest of the building, but there were long cupboards fixed to the walls with thick cream worktops to complement the dark wood doors. There was also a large avocado-coloured sink with shiny chrome taps. In the middle of the room were wide, gate-legged tables at which sat several old ladies and gentlemen on chairs with casters and high backs. One or two were painting a still life of flowers and fruit from an arrangement in front of them, using watercolours. Three other ladies appeared to be making cards with a selection of cut shapes, stickers, ribbons and glue.

There was original artwork on the walls, and Heather could smell a faint odour of linseed with which she was familiar from her own little studio room at home. Not that she was any good at painting, she was sure.

"Some of these are really skilful," Heather said, indicating the pictures.

"Residents have done those, and sometimes relatives are happy for us to keep them when the artist leaves us for a higher plane," Mary answered with tact. "That's the reality of working in a place like this, of course," she added quietly, so that only Heather could hear. "Although some do, there are other residents who don't always get to stay long."

Heather nodded soberly.

Windows looked out over a well-tended flower garden, where there was a glimpse of sunny daffodils and bright bedding plants. The curtains were made of thick cotton, brightly patterned with tones of red, orange and brown. Everything was comfortable, tasteful and affluent.

Mary approached a couple of elderly ladies seated in easy chairs in the corner of the room. Heather followed.

"How's it going, Evelyn?" Mary bent to look at the old lady's crochet. "Look at this, Heather. You are so skilful, Evelyn. Show our new recruit." Evelyn raised her work for Heather to see.

"Oh, a little jacket," Heather said to the lady in the comfy chair.

"It's for my great-granddaughter."

"I like the colour," Heather replied. "How old is the baby?"

"Only two months. She's called Naomi."

"How exciting. Congratulations. It must be lovely to know you have another generation in your family. Do they live close enough for you to see her?"

"Thank you, dear. Yes, they visit now and again. We like to sit here to knit, don't we, Beryl?" She turned to the other elderly resident. "We could go to the lounge, but it's so peaceful here, and Mary helps me if I drop a stitch. I can't see so easily these days."

"You're going to fit in very well here, Heather. I can tell already," Mary said as they straightened up.

"Everyone seems very friendly," Heather said. *Even the arrogant Will*, she thought. *Too friendly for my taste. I'll be fine so long as our paths don't cross too often.*

Since she was so busy, the day flew by. Heather didn't see Izzy, which was frustrating to say the least. She would have called by after her shift, but someone was helping her with a bath, so Heather contained her impatience until she could hear more of her story.

CHAPTER 4

"What *have* you done? You could do so much better. I wish you'd told me before you went," Brian said as he raised his half pint to his lips. "It's nothing like your work in the insurance office. You had some responsibility there, a team to respect you, a salaried position."

Yeah, and a bloke who cheated on me, not once but twice. A serial creep, Heather thought. *I had to leave. No way could I hang around and see him every day.* "I knew you'd disapprove. That's why I didn't say. It's a job. I need a job. I've got next to no money; I'm living at home again. Mum's been great, but I've been used to my own flat. There's hardly any work anywhere. You know people are queuing up for every job that's advertised."

"It'll be boring."

"But it'll keep me going while I'm looking around. Anyway, who knows? I might meet some rich old grandad who takes a fancy to me and leaves me his fortune before he kicks the bucket." She grinned wickedly and wrinkled her nose at him, knowing full well what his reaction to her statement would be.

"Heather, honestly! There's really no need for such talk." Brian was so predictable.

She sipped her Lambrusco and looked around the room. It was early, so the pub wasn't very full, although there was still a fug of smoke hanging near the ceiling. There was a gentle mumble of sound. Heather sighed and tossed her head.

"You could do with a haircut for that sort of place, too," Brian added, eyeing her mane of corkscrews as she pushed them away from her face. "At least make sure it's tied well back."

"For goodness' sake, Brian. Don't be such a snob." She gave him 'the look' and determined to ignore any snide remarks. He might be clever, but he clearly had no idea about the place at which she had been lucky enough to be taken on.

They'd been dating for four months. Almost four months of her knowing what Brian would say before he did. On the other hand, he was usually kind and very knowledgeable. They'd visited some great places, and he'd had loads of information to share when they did. He was a walking encyclopaedia. He was always the gentleman, and she felt safe and comfortable with him. She loved that about him; she did, really. She needed his consistency. Looking into his hazel eyes regarding her now, she pulled a moue and blew a kiss across the table. She liked how much he cared for her wellbeing. It still felt novel after the battering her self-esteem had taken with Kev.

"I wish you'd let me pull some strings at our place. I'm sure I can find you something there."

"No way," she answered, sitting back. "I'm not willing to let your manager try and touch me up whenever he comes into my sphere, like he tried at that office party you invited me to. I had enough of that with the oaf at the insurance office to last me a lifetime."

"I have to say, Heather, sometimes that's of your own making, you know. You must give off the wrong signals or something. You're too anxious to be liked. Maybe that's why you got hurt by whatever his name was."

"You mean Kev. Just say it." *God, he can sound so condescending sometimes*, she thought and looked down at her hands in her lap. She did have strong feelings for Brian, really, she did. It was true, she persuaded herself. He had rescued some of her confidence after the debacle with Kev, but she didn't need any reminders from him about it. She remained silent.

"Sorry," he said. "Shouldn't have brought that up."

"Never mind."

"You can stop looking at me with those big green eyes, too. You know I'm right."

She sighed.

"So, what's the next step with the job at the old peoples' home?" He changed the subject, trying to sound conciliatory.

"You mean The Beeches Care Home for the Elderly," she corrected him. "It's part of a group run by Crown, so it has a good reputation and looks after both independent people and those who need some specialist care. That's what the job ad said, anyway. When I went for the interview, I had a guided tour with the other candidates. I used the info I found at the library, and I must have said the right things during the interview." She shrugged.

"So, it's all arranged. You've done it. You could have told me before." Brian took another sip of his drink. "Oh, well, I only hope it's not as dull as it sounds."

"Brian! You're supposed to be supportive and encouraging."

"I am, really. You were the one who said it would only be until something better came along, though."

"I did, and it will," Heather stressed with a nod.

"I had a good time yesterday," Heather said as she grabbed her slice of toast and hurried around the table to pick up the mug of tea June had just finished pouring.

"I said you'd be fine. Now, sit down properly and eat your breakfast. You've always been able to talk to people and when you helped me out at that luncheon thing, the old folk loved chatting to you. What shift are you on today?"

"Not 'til ten o'clock, and then into the evening." She took a gulp from her mug as she sat down. "It's different from just chatting to people. I'm going to have to help these old dears with feeding, getting dressed, washing." She shrugged. "Brian said it would be boring, but it'll have to do for now. He said I should look for something better."

"Your Brian doesn't know what he's talking about."

"Mu-um! He's not *my* Brian … but he's usually right about things. He's very clever."

"Well, he knows nothing about old folk. It'll be a very rewarding job you've landed. You wait and see."

Mary was in the library this time. Heather asked Sue at reception where that might be, but evaded the suggestion that Will once more show her the way.

"No, no, I'll be fine. You've given me clear instructions," she said. She turned in the direction indicated and soon found where she was supposed to be.

"This is a beautiful room," she whispered, her eyes wide. All sound was muted, and the peach and grey furnishings gave a restful ambience.

"It's soundproofed in here and the armchairs are designed for the comfort of the elderly, of course."

"There are so many books. It's a real haven."

"Heather, come and say hello to Izzy. I think you two met the other day."

They crossed the thick carpet and Heather suddenly noticed the little lady swamped by the large wingback chair. "I didn't see you there," Heather said.

Izzy wore a lilac cardigan with a full skirt and blouse. Despite the warmth of the room, around her neck was a woolly scarf of a deeper shade of lilac. She had endeavoured to pull her grey hair back into a bun at the nape of her neck, but it was so fluffy that several strands always seemed to be escaping.

Heather crouched down to the side of her chair and smiled. "Hello again. It's Izzy Strong, isn't it? May I sit here for a moment? I don't want to disturb you, though, if it's not convenient."

As Heather glanced up, Mary backed off. Heather saw her gentle smile and encouraging nod. She was suddenly filled with confidence and warmth.

"Hello. Please do join me." Izzy nodded.

Heather took the chair next to her. "We met the other evening. I'm sure you remember. I'm Heather. May I call you Izzy?"

"Of course." She smiled.

Her eyes had the rheumy look of the elderly, with pink moistness showing beneath the bright blue, but they darted about and contained humour.

"What are you reading?" Heather spoke quietly with genuine interest. She knew she shouldn't be falsely jolly.

"It's a German novel. I had to ask for it especially."

"Not the regular request, I'm sure," Heather agreed.

"I learned the language as a child. Maybe I said? I can't remember. Then I spoke it a good deal between and after both wars."

"I remember you telling me that you had stayed in Germany between the wars." Heather had so many questions but just then, far away, she heard the mellow sound of a gong.

"Oh, good, I'm so hungry," Izzy said. Laying her book on a side table, she started to shuffle forwards with both hands on the arms of the chair. Heather noticed her long, delicate fingers. The skin was brown and the knuckles stood proud, with blue veins showing through the surface. Izzy wore a small ring with a tiny blue stone on her right hand but no other adornment. She struggled up onto her feet. Heather went to help her, but the old lady gave her a piercing look.

"No, dear, I must do this myself for as long as I can. I've always looked after myself and shall continue to do so." She looked at her surroundings and shrugged. "Even in this place."

Heather looked around the dining room and listened. There was a gentle buzz of sound and the meal smelled good. There was no odour of overcooked cauliflower or greens here like there had been at Heather's school.

Mary leaned in to whisper, "We always sit with the residents for lunch. You can see why." She nodded around her. "This is the highlight of the day for many of them, and we have a clear policy of ensuring it's a dignified time for those who find using cutlery or getting the food to their mouths difficult. It's important they enjoy it."

"I suppose it helps for them to see us staff as friendly and helpful, too. It seems a very modern idea from what I've read."

"Got it in one, Heather, excellent."

Unaccustomed delight caused Heather's smile to broaden when she received the praise. It had been sparse in her early life, and she had grown used to thinking little of herself.

"We must be sure to be ahead of the times, never mind keeping up. That's Eddie. Hi, Eddie." Mary waved at a man, and he waved a spoon and pulled back his lips to expose a gap-toothed grin.

"This is right good today, Mary," he replied, digging the spoon back into the bowl of stew before him.

"Do you want any of it cutting?"

"No, I'm good with it." He paused. "Maybe them carrots, though."

"This is Heather, she'll do it."

As Heather left her seat, she spotted Will across the room. He locked eyes with her, and she looked away hastily. As she bent to Eddie's plate, her insecurities and surety of Will's arrogance came to the fore. She was certain his eyes would be scanning her backside. She moved to stand sideways. She couldn't resist a quick glance as she stood upright again and straightened her T-shirt. The condescending smirk she saw on his face confirmed her previous idea.

Oh, honestly, she thought and tossed her hair as she turned her head away.

Heather gazed around the room, studiously avoiding that one area. No way was she going to be caught looking there again. Opposite her sat a man who had a serviette tucked into his collar, and someone was feeding him. One of the ladies had oddly shaped cutlery that turned at an angle, so she could manage on her own despite having little flexibility in her wrist. Some tables had more than one member of staff, and others had none. It appeared to depend upon the needs of the residents.

"I see you don't use bibs here," Heather observed, leaning towards Mary and speaking into her mentor's ear. "Some books I read in the library before my interview had illustrations that were very different to this."

"No, it's too demeaning. That's what I mean by treating everyone in a dignified way."

"It's not really treating everyone equally, is it? It's treating them differently, so they can be equal."

Mary's eyebrows raised almost imperceptibly. "How old did you say you were? That's very discerning of you."

"I'm twenty-five. Certainly no fledgling." Heather grinned.

As the meal finished and kitchen staff cleared away the dishes, the residents started to go their separate ways.

"Did you see how much Izzy Strong ate? You need to keep a discreet running record because she's a new resident, Heather," Mary said.

"I've just scribbled a note to myself to write up my daily diary before I go home tonight." Heather showed Mary the tiny notebook she had secreted in her pocket.

"That's excellent. You're going to be a real asset. Now, perhaps you would pop in on Izzy and see if she needs anything. Maybe she'd like to go to the craft room or down to the community room and watch some television. There's always the garden, of course."

Heather made her way to Izzy's room and found the old lady sitting in her chair. "Mary wondered if there are any activities you might like to investigate," she said.

"Come in, come in. No. That sort of thing isn't for me now. We could have a chat instead, unless you're busy."

"You'll have to tell me some more about your time in Germany. You had just met Garrit the other night. I hope you've had no more bad dreams."

"Not last night." Izzy gazed into the past.

CHAPTER 5

Berlin, 1927

"I'm trying such a lot of different things," Izzy said, as Gisela finished straightening her striped necktie. "When we went for coffee at the Kaiserhof I could never forget the splendour of those chandeliers and I enjoyed the Beethoven last night. It was quite amusing, watching Herr Furtwängler waving his baton so enthusiastically but, clearly, he has earned his reputation. I could almost *see* the music as it moved from one section of the orchestra to another."

"There's either great agitation or huge nobility with Beethoven."

"Yes, or much rage and amazing tenderness, but nothing in-between.."

"That's true. Right, I'm ready, are you?" Gisela turned from the mirror, and picking up her gloves she headed for the door. They were to meet several other young people at the gate to the *Zoologischer Garten* at three o'clock. "Kitty and Thelma are coming, I know, but which boys are coming is more to the point."

"Quite," Izzy answered, raising her eyebrows and tilting her head to one side in thought. "That is the big question. I think Max Achterberg will be there, from what he said. I wonder if Garrit will be there." She said the last as nonchalantly as she could, but Gisela was not fooled.

"Aha! I see where your brain is heading, or maybe your heart rather than your head. You do realise you talked an awful lot about him the other night," her friend crowed.

"Well, you have to admit he's charming."

"He's a bit on the dark side for my taste. Jewish blood, I imagine, especially with a name like Shain, but he seems a good egg," Gisela said.

Izzy looked sideways at her friend but said nothing. She was aware that there had been plenty of restless cultural and religious contradictions during and just after the war, so antisemitism, largely, had been integrated with these rather than standing out alone, but these days it was becoming more obvious to her. The rise of the German Fatherland Party in 1918 had not helped. Izzy knew that the national humiliation following the war and the astronomical sums of money the Germans were forced to pay in reparations had left its mark between the end of the war and now. She was curious and had read newspapers and books before she'd arrived, telling of high unemployment and hyperinflation. These conditions seemed to cause the people to search for someone to blame. Antisemitism had bubbled in Germany as an undercurrent, a marginal or localised phenomenon, for a very long time, as it had, she knew from her reading, across the globe. Here, the assassination of the Foreign Minister Herr Rathenau five years earlier was but one example. Now, she quite often heard comments about German nationalism and remarks against Jews in particular, and the Communists too, of course.

At the archway into the zoo, young people in colourful clothing were laughing and joking. Izzy scanned the group and felt oddly let down. Max's blond head was obvious above those of the other people. Kitty and Thelma were there, and a couple of people she had not met before. But no Garrit. She'd thought he was coming. He had indicated that he would. Now he wasn't here, and she experienced a sinking sensation that was hard to ignore.

They passed through the formal gardens towards the entrance to the zoo. Sometimes the men chased, and the girls giggled and screamed for effect. Older people looked on or dodged out of their paths with indulgent looks, tch-ing their teeth at the antics of the young.

"Come along, Izzy, where has your sunshine smile disappeared to?" Max took her hand and attempted to spin her around.

She made the effort for him.

"I know what will brighten your day, especially if you see it for the first time with me." His cheeks dimpled, and his eyes shone.

Izzy could not deny his handsome blond looks and decided to go with his flow. After all, if Garrit wasn't really that interested, a boy in her hand was worth... She turned on her most dazzling expression and danced along with him.

"There we are." Max waved his arm expansively. "What do you think of that?"

In front of them was the most ornate gateway she had ever seen. A matched pair of recumbent stone elephants guarded the portal, and as Izzy looked at the roofs over, and to each side, of the architecture, she took in their swooping lines and red, yellow and green stone. Above their heads, a huge Victorian-style triple lamp swung gently in the warm breeze. The wooden gates were open.

"Now, I agree," Izzy said. "That is very impressive."

"This is just the beginning. The animal houses within are just as grand, and some of the animals are exotic and truly astounding."

"I have been to a zoo before," she said.

"Ah, but not like this one," he pronounced. "This is the Berlin Zoo and not to be bettered, I'll be bound. We know how to do things well, here in Germany."

The park was truly amazing. They saw the bird house with its Indo-Gothic domed architecture. The birds within were colourful and exotic and very noisy with their demanding screeches. They saw a chimpanzee riding a little bicycle, which made Izzy laugh. There were massive tigers and a polar bear, which had quite a large pool in which to swim.

"The space these animals have is excellent," she said. "I went to a zoo at home, and they were in small cages where they just paced up and down all the time."

"This is a ground-breaking design and many of the animals produce young, not just the elephants, so they must be happy here. This is Germany for you," Max boasted. "We are a forward-thinking country, despite the penalties we have to pay. We will rise against tyranny."

"Indeed. That baby elephant was so, so endearing with the way it curled its little trunk around its mother's leg."

They were heading towards the Marble Hall for refreshment. Max and Izzy were holding hands and swinging along in front of the others. As they drew closer to the impressive building, Izzy was looking up at it and not at the crowd of people.

"Garrit, my fine fellow, what kept you?"

Izzy jumped as Max shouted and her gaze swung around. She felt her heart thumping.

"Hello, Max," Garrit said, touching his hat. "Izzy, hello. I see Max is taking care of you." His eyes dropped to their linked hands.

She promptly disengaged herself and felt her neck and cheeks grow warm.

"I was held up at home. Not of my own choosing," Garrit added, looking at Izzy. "I wondered if you might head this way, so I thought it would be the place to come. It's very busy here today. I'd have stood no chance of finding you all otherwise."

The rest of the group caught up, and there were general kisses and handshakes as they greeted each other. Having found a table which they could all fit around, Garrit managed to sit next to Izzy.

"You looked happy back there. I saw Max was looking after you," he said again to her now.

"Yes, he was. I thought you'd changed your mind about coming." She tossed her head and turned her face to the sun, closing her eyes. Now that he was here, perversely, she was annoyed with him. She sat for several moments, acutely aware of the buzz of voices but even more so of the silence next to her. When she finally opened her eyes, Garrit was watching her.

"I had to stay and help my mother with something very important. I could not possibly leave her to struggle alone. Father is out all day. He works so hard, you see, and such long hours with some of our poorer community. He gets very tired. I worry for his health. I feared I would not make it here at all but hurried all the way as soon as I was free."

The expression on his face was so tender and regretful that she took pity on him, but was reluctant for him to know that.

"Oh, well," she said with easy grace. Then she looked up at him from under her lashes and smiled her most bewitching smile as her sister, Delphi, would have done. Gradually she forgot to be coquettish and asked him about his family.

"My father is a doctor. Things are not easy for him, and my mother needs help with my younger sister. She cannot walk well. She has splints on her legs and her balance is poor. We have exercises that she must perform to strengthen her muscles, but she needs help with those."

"Does she live with you, then?"

"Yes. Several people said, when she was born, that she should go to an institution but my father, as a doctor, said no. That was no place for her. She would be left to degenerate with no stimulus. She is clever. She just has difficulty moving. You would like her. She is fun and laughs a lot at her own misfortune."

Izzy looked at him steadily. His face was animated and his eyes sparkled when talking of his little sister. "I should like to meet her," she said.

"Oh, you must. That would be marvellous. She has few visitors. She would love to see you." He paused. "Perhaps you would come to our house and take some afternoon refreshment. We have tea, you know." He smiled at her and his face crinkled in the most devastating manner.

"That would be enchanting," Izzy replied.

"We will fix a date before we leave here."

On returning to Gisela's house, Izzy found a letter waiting for her. It was from her papa.

"I haven't heard from him for a while," she said to her friend.

"He is coping on his own, isn't he?" asked Gisela.

"I think so. I can hardly believe it's been so long since Mama's passing." Izzy sighed.

"I suppose her resistance was low, so she just couldn't fight the influenza at the end of the war. I believe that's what *Mumie* said."

"Mmm." Izzy tore open the flimsy paper. "Oh no!" She spun around and brandished the letter in the air.

"What is it?"

"I am to return home," she wailed.

"Is something wrong with your papa?" Gisela sometimes struggled to speak English, but Izzy responded in perfect, if slightly accented, German.

"No, not really, but my sister is now definitely coming from Australia and Papa wants me back. Honestly, she always did have the knack of getting her own way and upsetting everyone, and she's still managing it, even from Australia." She read on. "Also, my other sister, Rose, has been in hospital." Her voice grew higher.

"Did you not know that? Were you not told?"

"Papa never said. Why didn't he say? Ah…" She paused as she read further. "Oh Lord. She has tuberculosis. Oh, this is dreadful. I've been having such fun and she has been so ill."

"But you didn't know. He must have been protecting you. Is she recovering? The rate is much better now."

"Yes, she's much improved, apparently, and out of immediate danger. She's in a sanatorium. I will have to go home. I don't want to, but I must see Rose. And poor Papa."

"I don't want you to go either. What will Rose say about Delphi returning? Didn't you say she and Delphi didn't get along?"

"Rose? I can't imagine she'll be too pleased about it, but knowing Rose she'll be welcoming. Mind you, I never really knew exactly what went on between the two of them. I was considered a bit too young to be told, and then Delphi went away and we all just got on with life."

"What? You never got the whole story?" Gisela was astounded.

"No, not really. I know there was some dreadful row between Rose and Delphi, but the focus was on Delphi expecting a baby and skipping off to Australia with her lover's parents. That was all pretty risqué back then. Well, it still is, of course. The story is that her 'husband' died in France. That's nearly true, though. He did die there. Not quite her husband, that's all. There. Now you know all our secrets."

"And you never asked Rose what the great falling out was about?"

"Yes, I asked. I was never told, that's all. Gisela, for goodness' sake, stop asking all these questions. It's family business. So … no more, and don't you dare go blabbing about it." Izzy sat heavily. Then her own situation returned to the fore. "I don't want to leave right now. Things are just getting interesting. I'm to go to Garrit's house and meet his sister. Why is life never easy?"

CHAPTER 6

Yorkshire, 1975

Heather's heart leaped. She took a huge gulp of air and held onto the door handle to steady herself. She'd opened the door to the office and found Will skulking inside. There was no other word for it. He looked shifty as he straightened up and made out he hadn't been reading a paper that lay on the desk. He proceeded to replace it in a folder, and put the folder on a pile to one side. He closed the lid of a small cash box that lay next to it and swished a duster around.

At midday Mrs Friend, the matron who managed the whole place, had approached Heather. "You couldn't possibly do a double shift, could you? One of the others has gone home sick. You can have a free meal here and you'll get time and a half, of course. It'll mean a very long day, though, I'm afraid."

"I could, yes," Heather had shrugged. "I've nothing else on tonight, but perhaps I could just phone my mum and let her know. Otherwise she'll have dinner on."

"Of course. Use the phone in my office."

She had gone straight there to do just that.

"What are you doing here?" She watched Will's face closely for his reaction.

"I came to do my job. I'm emptying the bins. I might ask you the same question."

"I've permission to use the phone, but I shan't be snooping about while I'm here," she said with as much chill as she could muster. "Much in the cash box, was there?"

"No idea. I was closing it for security. Aren't you Miss Perfect, then?" He picked up the wastepaper basket and emptied it into a black plastic sack, before flicking the duster around some more and leaving.

How audacious, Heather thought. *How utterly untrustworthy, and they all think he's wonderful. He clearly can't be relied upon.*

Then doubt set in, always sitting at her shoulder.

Should I tell? I didn't see him take anything. I wonder what he was looking at, and why? I'll not be well thought of if I accuse wonder-boy when I'm still so new. Perhaps I'll just keep my eyes open where he's concerned. She moved across to ensure the door was ajar, then made her phone call, not wanting to be accused of anything inappropriate while she was in there.

It was late when Heather finally left The Beeches and headed round the building for her bike. Each light outside cast a small glowing circle on the tarmac beneath, but the spaces between were dim and shadowed. As she bent to undo the lock, she was sure she heard someone clear their throat. She suddenly felt nervous. Narrowing her eyes at the bushes, she cast about. All she could see were shadows, and all she heard was rustling. Maybe it was just the breeze in the beech trees' branches.

She started to relax and returned her attention to her bike.

Snap. It sounded like a twig cracking.

"Who's there?" She whispered into the dark, a chill tickling her spine. She flattened herself against the wall of the building. Then she felt a little ridiculous and thought, it's probably just a cat.

"Shh!" A disconnected sound came from within the foliage.

"What? Who's there? Stop messing about. I'll shout out if you're up to no good," she said, trying to sound cool but feeling her heart thump. Had someone crept in from the spinney beyond the bushes? Were they casing the joint or waiting to pounce on unsuspecting staff?

Bending to her bike lamp, she unclipped it and shone it into the dark towards the sound.

"Turn that bloody thing off," said a voice she recognised. "You'll blind me and scare them off."

There was much rustling and cursing, and after a moment Will emerged from the bushes, looking less than happy.

"Oh, for goodness' sake. It's you! Scare who off?"

"The badgers. It's an ancient sett, in there." He nodded over his shoulder. "I've been observing them and making notes for weeks. They won't show themselves now, with all this light and crashing around."

This new information about Will surprised Heather, and it took the wind out of her sails. Then she remembered how scared she had been a moment previously, how she had caught him looking guilty in Mrs Friend's office, and how similar to Kev he looked.

She resolved not to give ground, so she snapped at him. "Well, I didn't know who was skulking around in the bushes at this time of night. You're clearly good at sneaking about. Lots of practice." She paused. "And you didn't have to shush me like a naughty kid, either," she added to maintain her dignity.

He sighed. "OK, I suppose you weren't to know. It's just that I think there could be cubs, and I've been waiting for days to see them come out. There weren't any last year, although I'm sure I saw a pregnant female."

"Why was that? No cubs last year, I mean." Heather's curiosity got the better of her.

"Sometimes they die underground and never emerge from the nesting chamber; maybe if food and water are scarce. Last year, we had that hot dry spell just around Easter. Perhaps that was it."

"You're expecting to see them now, are you?" She was interested but determined to maintain her spiky attitude.

"I thought I saw a nose poking out of the hole a couple of nights ago. It looked too small for an adult, and it's about the right length of time since I saw the female last."

"Don't they smell you being so close?"

"Thanks, I'm not that bad," he said and laughed.

Heather caught what she took to be a smirk on his face and she retreated. "All very interesting, I'm sure, but you shouldn't go hiding in the bushes like that. What if one of the residents came by? They could have a heart attack."

"Firstly, no residents would come around here. Secondly, they'll be getting tucked up or watching TV at this time of night, and thirdly they all know I've been keeping a diary for a couple of years on the badgers."

This last, of course, was news to Heather. "Time I was off. I'm shattered," she said, and without risking a further glance at Will she finished undoing the combination on her bike lock and slung the helmet over the handlebars so that she could make a quick getaway.

"You ought to put that on your head," Will said, nodding at the helmet. "No point having it and not wearing it, especially in the dark."

She knew he spoke sense. "I hate it. Ugly new-fangled thing. Never had them as kids," she said. "I seriously doubt it would do any good if I fell off." She pedalled away, thinking she would stop at the end of the drive once out of his sight and put it on anyway.

Honestly, the cheek of the man; such a know-all, she thought as she left. And I *know* he's not to be trusted.

She did stop and fasten the offending headgear under her chin before she left the driveway, though. Turning her head just before cycling off again, she was annoyed to see Will was still standing under one of the lights, watching her departure.

"You haven't waited up for me, have you?" Heather said to her mum when she got home.

"Not really," June replied, turning to the kettle and lighting the gas under it. "Fancy a cup of tea?"

"Certainly would," Heather said with feeling.

"You must be shattered, pet, after a double shift. Sit down. It won't be long. I thought you'd have been in a bit before this."

"I was just leaving when that caretaker guy gave me a right start."

"What do you mean?"

"He was skulking around in the bushes near where I'd left my bike."

"What on earth for?"

Heather told her mum about the badger sett and of the cubs that should be emerging.

"Well, he can't be all bad if he's into wildlife to that extent," June said.

"I must admit I was quite surprised. Apparently, he's been keeping a diary for about two years."

"Blimey, that's a long time. He sounds quite a nice chap. From what you said, the residents and other staff like him well enough."

"Mmm, but he's arrogant and he reminds me of Kev with his blond hair and his dimply smile." *And he was ferreting about in the office*, she thought, but she chose not to say that out loud. She wasn't sure why.

"Ah, I see," said her mum. "Oh dear."

The next day Heather was detailed to help Izzy again, not that she needed much help. Mainly she liked to talk and if prompted, she might divulge more of her early life, Heather hoped. It was all so fascinating, especially since her own grandmother lived abroad, in Spain. Izzy seemed to have led a very full life. It sounded as if something mysterious had gone on somewhere along the way. She still hadn't heard about any wire or a wall.

"Shall I brush your hair for you? I can make it into a bun too."

"My sister Rose used to brush my hair when I was young," Izzy said. "She always had such a gentle touch." She passed the brush to Heather.

"Was Rose older than you?"

"Yes, nearly five years older. She was always the peacemaker. Not like Delphi. I used to share a bedroom with Rose so Delphi could have her own. She was the wild one. Typical middle sister. I suppose I became quite wayward too, in Germany, for a time. Things were so different there. More relaxed and easy-going. My friend Gisela and I had a rare old time. When the summons came for me to return to England, I was far from pleased."

"What do you mean?" Heather was curious. "Why was it a summons?"

"That was Delphi, of course. Even from the other side of the world she had the power to disrupt. It came naturally to her."

"Oh dear," Heather said, trying to be tactful. "Did you go home? And did you see Garrit at his home and meet his sister before you left?"

"I did, and that was a surprise."

CHAPTER 7

It was several nights later before Heather saw Brian again. He had been away on a course, but the phone rang almost as soon as she got in from work on the afternoon of his return.

"I thought we could go to that newish pub tonight, the one that reopened on the corner a couple of months ago. See what it's like," he said.

She stood winding the curly wire around her fingers as she answered. "Yes, okay, but I don't want to be out late. I'm on an early shift tomorrow."

"I'll pick you up at eight-thirty, then?"

"That'll give us an hour or so."

"Is that all? How early is early? I haven't seen you for days." He sounded impatient.

Heather bit her bottom lip. "Can you come at seven?"

"Right. I'll see you then."

The pub was already quite busy, and a cloud of smoke hung just below the falsely beamed ceiling. The noise, as soon as they opened the door, was deafening. There was a jukebox in the corner, playing 'Listen To What The Man Said'. They pushed their way through the throng.

"You grab a table while I get them in. Your usual?" Brian worked his way through to the bar.

Heather found a corner and managed to rearrange a couple of stools for them. She hummed contentedly along to the music as she watched Brian carefully balance her glass and a half pint for himself with a couple of packets of crisps.

As he sat, she dutifully asked him about his course. Then she said, "I've had an interesting few days too."

"What? At the old peoples' home?"

"At the care home, yes."

"Honestly, Heather, it's really not a career, is it?"

She gave up.

Someone must have put a coin in the jukebox, because 10CC's 'I'm Not in Love' came on.

"I sometimes wonder what Mum saw in my dad. He was such a control freak."

"What on earth brought that on?"

"Oh, um, the words of that song, I suppose," Heather said with speed. "He came up in conversation the other day too, when I was telling Mum about this resident we have. She went to Germany all on her own when she was my age." Heather finally told him what little she had gleaned so far about Izzy.

"From what you've told me, your dad ruled you with a rod of iron. There's protection and there's intimidation, if you ask me," Brian said. "Why didn't your mum stand up to him a bit?"

"Anything for a quiet life, I think. It's easier said than done, too. She always said she was okay with it. I'm guessing she didn't want to add to an unpleasant atmosphere for me," Heather said, staring ahead.

"*He's* why you're so bad at decision-making." Brian nodded at her.

"I'm not that bad," she said. *Probably why I can't settle with the right man, though*, she thought to herself. *Either I branch out, trying to be a rebel, and they lead me a right dance with their cheating, or they're a bit on the dull, safe side and think they know everything. Never in-between. Thanks, Dad. It's true, you were a rotten role model.* "We had to be so careful about everything," Heather continued aloud. "I remember one time. I must have been about thirteen. I forgot to put a newspaper on the table under my writing. He blew his top, of course, and told me I'd be leaving imprints in the wood."

"I suppose he had a point. Trying to keep stuff in good order," Brian said.

Heather raised her eyebrows and stared at him. "I went mad. I completely lost it and screamed at him. I was so fed up with his pernickety attitude. I'd never done that before and not since, either. I slammed out of the room and ran upstairs. I remember when I banged my door shut an ornament fell off the shelf."

"Wow, what happened?"

"Mum came up and we talked. She kind of stood up for him. She said it would be easiest for everyone if I went downstairs and apologised. It was soon after that he left."

"Maybe he could see the worm was turning."

"What do you mean?" Heather frowned at Brian.

"Well, perhaps he was worried he wasn't going to be able to rule you for much longer."

"Oh, I don't know. It was good riddance, anyway," she said.

"I think it's probably had a lasting effect on you, though." Brian sipped his beer and Heather shrugged. "There you are," he said.

"What?"

"Shrugging your shoulders as if you want to bury what I say, so you don't have to consider it. And you didn't listen to me when I suggested a better job at my place."

"Oh, Brian, don't start that again. Anyway, I thought you wanted me to be more decisive."

He looked at her with raised eyebrows and his head on one side. She felt small again. "Don't get into an argument with me," he said. "Do you want another?" He nodded at her glass.

"Thank you," she answered, and as he pushed his way through the throng she sighed. *Me, get into an argument? It wasn't me*, she thought. *Blimey, he's sounding a bit like my dad.*

When he returned, though, he suggested going for a drive out into the hills on Saturday and finding a cosy pub for lunch.

Dad would never have suggested that, she thought. *No, he's not like my dad at all.*

When Heather got home from her shift just after lunch the following day, she had a shock. She'd put her bike in the shed, taken off her helmet and was looking forward to a lazy cup of tea and a sit in the kitchen, chatting with her mum. They might watch that Des O'Connor thing later on, and then *The Rockford Files*. He was dishy, that James Garner. He had a quirky, wicked smile.

She pushed open the kitchen door. The sun outside was so bright it took her a minute to notice that a pair of long jean-clad legs and a very neat backside were kneeling on the floor, with the top half hidden in the cupboard under the sink.

"Hello," she said. The back reared up and there was a clunk and a swearword as, presumably, the man's head hit the pipework inside the cupboard. "I'm so sorry. I didn't mean to make you jump."

The body wriggled, a naked torso emerged and then… Heather's heart leaped. It was Will.

"You! What the hell are you doing here?"

Will rubbed his scalp. "Fixing a leak for your mum."

"Why you?" She regarded his chest, brown from the sun and with fair hair barely covering a fine set of pectoral muscles. His jeans hung low and a strip of blond hair descended in a line beneath the waistband. She raised her eyes immediately.

"Mary at The Beeches offered my services. Apparently she knows a friend of your mother's, Deidre, I think but I hadn't realised your surname was Rawson. So, when Mary asked me if I'd help out this friend of a friend of hers..." He shrugged.

"What?" Heather was thrown into confusion. "Oh, I see. Right. I have to..." Heather pointed at the hallway and made a dive for the door to go and find her mum.

"Why is *he* doing it?" she hissed as soon as she had tracked down her parent.

"What on earth do you mean? Mary said she knew just the person when I told her about the drippy pipe under the sink. I met her in town yesterday. We had a coffee. Didn't I say?"

"No, you didn't. That's Will. From The Beeches. The arrogant pest. The caretaker bloke. The one who can't be trusted."

"Oh, darling, really. You told me he hadn't pestered you, and he seems very charming. What do you mean, 'can't be trusted'? He's certainly doing us a favour for a very reasonable price. Next to nothing, really. Go and put the kettle on, there's a honey. I just need to finish this letter to your Aunty Gill."

The sense of being trapped was almost overwhelming. Heather scouted around for an excuse not to return to the kitchen. "I, um. How was your day?" She did her best to sound casual.

"Make a cup of tea, and then I'll have finished this. I'll come through to the kitchen and all three of us can have a sit down. Our knight will be ready for a cup by then, I should think."

There was no alternative. Heather wandered back down the hallway.

"Tea or coffee?" she asked. She sounded sullen and rude, even to her own ears.

"Tea, please. Thanks. That'd be great," he replied from under the sink. Heather watched, mesmerised as his bottom wiggled again and he emerged from the cupboard. "That should do it. I need to turn the water back on. Let's hope for the best."

She glared at him.

"Look, I don't know what I've done that's so awful in your eyes," he said.

"Really? How about smirking at me at every opportunity? How about sneaking around and prying, and … and…" She finished on a feeble note.

"I wasn't stealing anything in the office the other day, you know."

"Whatever you say."

"I'd heard that a…"

"Have you finished?" Heather's mother breezed in. "You are a star. Thank you so much. It's that sort of job that's too tricky for me."

"I'll just turn the water back on to check it's done properly." He knelt and reached into the cupboard to turn the tap. After a moment, he said, "Seems fine."

"Thank you again. Please, sit there and Heather will have the tea ready, won't you, darling?"

Heather huffed and turned back to the kettle as Will reached to retrieve his shirt from the back of a chair.

Izzy was in the library again, the next time they met. "You're looking lovely today," Heather said. "That colour suits you. Are you not too hot with your scarf on, though? It's a lovely day outside."

"So I see," the old lady answered. "I came to retrieve my book. I thought I might venture out. Perhaps you might accompany me? Unless, of course, you have other matters to which you must attend."

She has a funny old-fashioned turn of phrase, Heather thought. *But then she is old and kind of quaint in her lilac cardigan and woolly scarf, even in early summer.*

Izzy retrieved her walking stick, gave Heather her book to carry with its blue tasselled bookmark, and tucked her hand through her arm. "There we are. We're fit to go. That's cosy."

They exchanged a smile and slowly moved towards the garden.

There were a couple of comfy-looking chairs in the shade of one of the beech trees. Heather noted that the metal was newly repainted. The cushions were patterned with huge yellow, white and green flowers.

"These are perfect," Izzy said as she settled back. "I think Will has been busy on them. He does seem a good, hardworking boy."

"Mmm. Maybe," was all Heather could muster.

"Don't you like him?" Izzy fixed her with a twinkling gaze, causing Heather to lower her eyes.

"I don't think I quite trust him."

"Really?"

The silence elongated until Heather was compelled to speak. "I found him rifling through papers on Mrs Friend's desk the other day. He was shifty about it. And there was a petty cash box there."

"Oh dear. Did you tell anyone?"

"No. He told me he wasn't stealing, and I'm not sure who would believe me if I started telling tales. But all the same..."

"Perhaps on this occasion we'll let it lie," Izzy said. "I heard he has troubles at home. We don't want to add to it. Dishonesty has a way of revealing itself if the person is given enough leeway. We'll keep an eye open and our ears to the ground, so to speak."

"Troubles?" Heather asked.

"Yes. It reminds me of Garrit and his situation. That was a terrible thing for his poor mother."

Heather's attention was diverted.

CHAPTER 8

Berlin, 1927

Izzy held the piece of paper in her hand with Garrit's address. He had said he would come to meet her somewhere, but she had insisted on being independent. At the back of her mind was the thought that Gisela's parents might not be entirely happy for her to be meeting him. There seemed to be an atmosphere in the house every time someone or something to do with Jewishness was mentioned. In the end, she had not needed to negotiate public transport. She had told Gisela what she was doing, confident that she would have an ally. She had therefore travelled to the east of the city in the back of the chauffeured car belonging to Gisela's father and now, here she was, in Prenzlauer Berg. Garrit had told her that he was just around the corner from the Carl Legion buildings in Erich-Weinert Strasse.

Izzy's thick, bobbed hair, in the latest style, fell forward from under her hat as she leaned to speak to the driver. "We must be close now."

"Yes, miss. Round the next corner." With that, he pulled up outside a tall building with cream-coloured walls, windows that wrapped around the corner, and curved balconies on each floor. All quite modern-looking. She glanced at her piece of paper as the chauffer arrived and came around to her door.

She felt very grand arriving like this. Gisela's father was affluent, she knew, but to be treated like royalty was still a luxury, even though the friends had travelled together this way several times before. The chauffeur had already dropped Gisela off in the centre of the city. She was more than happy to have an afternoon shopping with another friend while Izzy was having tea at Garrit's house. It was only a minor omission that had led her father to believe they would be together for the whole afternoon. Gisela had been a complete brick to arrange it all, on the firm understanding that Izzy would give her all the gossip when she returned.

"You know if Papa knew who you were visiting, he would not be best pleased. That district is nice enough, but a lot of Jews live there. Really, you are being very headstrong, Izzy. It's just as well you are leaving for home soon. Still, this mild flirtation won't hurt in the time you have left, so long as you tell me all about it. I'd love to know what the inside of a Jew's house is like. I mean do they live like us?" Gisela had mused.

"I'm sure they are exactly 'like us', as you put it. His father is a doctor, you know." Izzy had been unimpressed by the tone her friend had taken.

"Just ensure you give me all the *schmooze*, as Garrit himself might say." Gisela had laughed heartily.

Now, Izzy stepped down off the running board as the car door was opened. She asked the chauffeur to return in two hours.

"Yes, miss." He touched his cap.

Leaves on the trees opposite rustled in the breeze, becoming dry as they did in autumn. Tiny flowers livened up the grass. It was a beautiful day; the sort of day that sang to your soul.

Izzy brushed down her skirt at the back. Her caramel linen dress was set off with cream piping, forming a deep V shape from the shoulders, and around the dropped waist. A double coloured bow with ribbons on one shoulder, in just the correct shades, finished off the design. A long double string of pearls complemented her outfit, and a little cloche hat with a cream rose-shaped trim was perfect on her short hair. She really did feel quite the thing. As she approached the main door, Garrit opened it to welcome her with a beaming smile which animated his whole demeanour, and Izzy's heart gave a little lurch. Oh, he was so handsome, and charming, too.

He held out both his hands to her. "My dear, I'm so pleased and indeed privileged to welcome you to my home. I saw you arriving." With that, he leaned in and kissed her on each cheek. His proximity made her heart skip, and her breath became short as she felt his cheek against her own and smelled his masculinity.

He was watching out and waiting for me, she thought with a ripple of pleasure.

"As you see, we are quite humble, even though my father is a doctor of medicine. We're very lucky to have one of these new modern apartments, though. My mother is looking forward to meeting you, and Ester, my sister, is very excited. She has spoken of little else. Any visitors are a highlight for her. Come, I'm talking too much." He laughed at himself in a disarmingly self-deprecating manner. He held the door for her to precede him and indicated the stairs leading up to the first floor.

"*Mutti*, this is my friend, Izzy."

His mother came forward and held out her fingers to take Izzy's hand. She was small and dark-haired, and wore good-quality clothes. She was also very genteel and good-looking in a sparrow-like way.

"And this is my sister, Ester."

The girl grinned and Izzy nodded at her and said, "I'm pleased to meet you."

"Please take a seat," Garrit's mother said before Izzy could approach Ester.

Izzy had the opportunity to glance around while Frau Shain said she would fetch the refreshments. The floor tiles were very Art Deco, but the furnishings were more traditional and in heavy dark wood. There was a chaise longue covered in russet velvet under the window, and several chairs covered in dark brown leather were grouped around a low table. A few paintings adorned the pale ochre walls. One, in a heavy gold frame, was of an older lady dressed in black bombazine, and her hair was scraped back into a severe bun.

Garrit caught Izzy's gaze and said, "My great-grandmother. She looks a little fierce, don't you think? I never met her. I think she would have been a very determined lady."

A piano stood at one end with its lid up and a piece of music open on the rest.

"Do you play, Ester?" Izzy sat opposite Garrit's sister. Ester shook her head. It was then that Izzy saw the girl's arm, with its hand curled at an odd angle. It seemed Ester could not control its movement. Izzy was shocked; she had been unaware of the extent of her problems. "I imagine you like to listen, though," she said. Then she noticed the girl's legs and understood. It was Little's disease, although Izzy thought that perhaps these days it was called cerebral palsy. That must be what Ester had.

"I think if I played the *Moonlight Sonata* it would sound more like Wagner's *Valkyrie*." She laughed as she held up her waving hand. "Except with all those notes in the wrong order, too."

"Sometimes we play a duet, don't we?" Garrit said, and there was fondness on his face as he looked across at his sister.

"You play and I add the odd note here and there." Ester smiled back at him.

Frau Shain re-appeared, and Izzy leaped up. "May I help you?"

"Certainly not on your first visit here." She smiled, which took the sting from the sharpness of her words, but Izzy had the uncomfortable thought that Frau Shain may have inherited some fierceness from the lady in the painting.

Tea was passed, as were small plates for a range of tiny pastries and cakes.

"So, my dear, Izzy. Have you known my son long?"

"Not so long, and I fear I have to return to England soon. My sister is coming back from Australia, where she has been for almost ten years. I am certain I should like to revisit Berlin. It's such an exciting and vibrant city."

"Yes, indeed it is. There is much art and design and freedom here, although things are not always easy for such as us. We have a strict culture of our own, do we not, Garrit? We must follow our own rules and religion. Garrit knows this."

Izzy looked at her. Was this a warning to her? She was not Jewish as they were. Was Frau Shain letting her know what her position was to be in relation to her son?

"Not so much these days, *Mutti*," Garrit said, which earned him a strange look from his mother, but she said no more on that subject.

The rest of Izzy's time passed pleasantly enough. She had a long conversation with Ester about her interest in collecting and pressing wildflowers, and Izzy could not deny Frau Shain was courteous and friendly.

When it was time for her to leave, she shook hands and thanked her hostess. Garrit led her down the stairs to the front entrance. "I wondered if you would accompany me to one of the films that we have here in Berlin, before you depart. Our film industry is thriving, as I'm sure you know."

Izzy grinned and clapped her hands. "That would be so exciting. I should love to. I'll be here for a little while longer. My sister has still to arrange her voyage, and that will take some weeks."

"There is a film that you might consider to be too outrageous, but it's an important one to me." He went on to describe it. "It portrays a pogrom which is carried out against the Jewish inhabitants of a village in Tsarist Russia. In the background there is a love story between a young Russian soldier student and the daughter of the leader of the Jewish community, something that is a bit risqué, so if it is not for us…"

"It sounds serious, but very interesting," Izzy said and nodded with determination. "When might we go?"

"I have my work to complete, but since most of that is done here at home, I can fit other things in my life quite easily."

"Oh? What do you do?"

"I translate. Since I speak three languages as well as German, I have enough to keep me busy. The Friedrich Wilhelm Universität has the medical campus, and they give me technical papers to translate. If I get stuck, I can ask my father's advice. It works well. I can be here to help *Mutti* and Ester, too. What about Tuesday of next week?"

"That would indeed be wonderful." Izzy's driver arrived. "Oh, here's my transport. Where shall I meet you?"

"In the vestibule of the Gloria-Palast? It's in Charlottenburg. I wonder if that is better for you than me coming to call at the house where you are staying. I understand that Gisela's father is quite…"

"Yes, I know, and yes, that's perfect. I shall meet you there. I know it. I think it's much closer to where I'm living than to you."

They decided the time and Izzy took her leave.

"*Tschüss mein lieblingsmädchen*," said Garrit.

All the way home, she hugged his words to her heart. *My favourite girl. Truly? Oh, my.* His mother's words also hung in the air, though, like a heavy rebuke.

CHAPTER 9

Yorkshire, 1975

"It takes a long time to truly know another," Izzy said.

Heather was mentally still in Berlin, enchanted by Izzy's words. *My favourite girl*, she thought. *How romantic.* She dragged her mind back to the present. "I suppose so," she answered vaguely.

Izzy shivered.

"Are you getting a bit chilly out here? Shall we go in?"

"Yes, I think so."

The leaves of the ancient copper beech tree above their heads trembled in the breeze, and Heather realised the shade had become quite cool.

Izzy manoeuvred herself forward in her chair. Heather waited, respecting her independence. The older lady arose, after which she stood still for a moment.

"I just need to get my balance before moving off." She gave a little laugh and shook her head. "It's very frustrating getting old," she said. "Let's link arms."

"I think your determination will keep you young," Heather said, and Izzy patted her hand.

Heather matched her pace to Izzy's, and together they ambled towards the doors to the home, open and welcoming.

"What would you like to do now? How about the craft room? Mary will suggest some activity you may enjoy."

Izzy gave her an old-fashioned look. "I don't need to be organised into activities, young lady. I'm not quite in my dotage yet."

Heather laughed. "No, of course not. Sorry."

Old, she might be, but still strong in spirit. Like her second name, Heather mused. She was deep in thought about this when Izzy spoke again.

"Still, I might like to have a look at the craft room. I haven't explored much yet."

They got the lift to the first floor and found the door to the craft room open.

"Hello, Izzy," Mary said. "Why don't you have a look around and see the kind of things we do? There are some examples on the walls, or some unfinished things are on the side over there."

As Heather drifted away to give Mary and Izzy some space, she heard Mary say, "We don't try and organise our residents. It's entirely up to you what you do or want to explore…"

Heather smiled to herself, and she was still smiling when she turned the corner of the L-shaped room and almost fell over Will, who was standing with his back to her, gazing at a photograph on a small table to his side. An easel stood in front of him and a filbert brush was poised in his hand. She recognised the shape as being a favourite of painters for its versatility, as in her own dabbling. She came to an abrupt halt, but he appeared so engrossed in his work that he didn't see her, giving her the opportunity to survey him while she dithered about what to do. Should she turn and hurry away? Mary would think it odd, and she had to hang around and wait for Izzy to decide what she wanted to do next. She stood her ground.

It looked like Will was painting a portrait, but she couldn't see properly. His shoulders were shielding the painting from sight. As she inhaled the familiar smell of linseed, she knew he was painting in oils. She had made no sound, but just then he altered his position and caught sight of her. As she forced her gaze away from his work, their eyes met, and his mouth rose at the corner. A deep dimple appeared in his left cheek.

"Are you spying on me, Heather Rawson?"

"Certainly not."

"Because if you were, I'd have to kill you. This isn't finished yet and it's going to be a gift for someone, so it's a secret."

Heather couldn't keep the grin from her face. Then she thought better of a light response. He didn't deserve it. After all, he was a sneak thief. "If you choose to spend your working time painting, that's entirely up to you and your boss," she sniped.

"'Appen I'll manage," he fired off, his local accent coming to the fore, "if you decide to tell on me."

Without giving him the chance to say anything else, Heather tossed her hair, spun around and headed back to Izzy and Mary.

"Did you find Will around there?" Mary said. "He comes here when he has a spare hour or two between shifts, usually on a Tuesday. Stella goes to the workshop on Tuesdays."

Heather didn't follow this at all and was about to ask who Stella was, when Izzy said, "I think I'd like to go back to the library now, if that's alright. I would rather like to read another chapter before teatime. Thank you, Mary."

Thoughts of Will and his painting disappeared as they headed down to the library. Izzy chatted about what she had seen in the craft room.

Heather settled the old lady, making sure she was comfortable, then fetched her book. "Can I get you a drink or anything?"

"Just a glass of tap water would be good. There's a jug over there, look."

"I'll see you tomorrow, Izzy. I hope you sleep well."

"Oh, I'm sure I'll be alright, come what may. Enjoy your own evening, my dear."

Heather walked back along the corridor with a view to heading home when her heart overtook her brain. What was Will painting? The glimpse she'd had stirred her curiosity until she could bear it no longer, and she hurried back along the corridor to the craft room. The thick carpet deadened her tread, although it was highly unlikely anyone else would be in this area by now. They had all been in the process of packing away. Tea was imminent and Will himself would be on duty elsewhere by now, of that she was sure.

Pushing open the door, she peeped around. Seeing it was indeed empty, she quickened her pace across the room. Will's easel stood with a muslin cloth covering his work. Heather's heart beat a little faster. She paced back and forth a couple of times, trying to decide whether she should look or not, now she was here in front of the painting. She rubbed her hands together and fiddled with the locket which hung on a chain around her neck.

To lift the cloth on Will's painting would be an intrusion. But she couldn't resist. A small peep wouldn't hurt. She lifted a corner and saw delicate brush strokes depicting fabric in a mint green, with blue and orange stitching picked out with undeniable skill. Heather knew she should look no further, but the glimpse made it irresistible. With guilt, she banished her scruples and raised the fabric further to reveal the whole painting. A portrait of a girl with red flyaway hair and vivid, green eyes stared back at her. She stepped sideways and the eyes followed her. The whole had a Pre-Raphaelite look and reminded her of Dante Gabriel Rossetti's *Fiammetta*, only instead of being surrounded by roses, this portrait had leaves and berries still at the sketched stage. Although unfinished, it was clearly a work of genuine skill.

Heather stood mesmerised until a sound in the distance brought her to her senses, and she quickly replaced the cloth. She scouted around with haste to see if the picture from which he was painting was still around. Sometimes photos had identification of the subject scrawled on the back. There was no sign of it.

Was this his girlfriend? The portrait was of a girl, almost too young for that, surely, but she could not be certain. She was stunningly pretty. As Heather turned away, she was suddenly cross. Her reaction puzzled her. Then she thought, *How dare he flirt with me when he has this lovely girl hidden somewhere.* Why was she always attracted to this type of man? What was it they did for her?

Just as she was turning from the painting, she heard the door open. Her heart raced. She was tempted to duck down behind the easel, but she realised it would be highly embarrassing to be caught doing that. Instead, she straightened her shoulders and turned to see who had come in.

It wasn't Will or even Mary who approached so quietly across the linoleum floor. It was Izzy.

They were both as surprised as the other, it seemed, to meet here. "Oh, hello, dear." Izzy took a small step back and put her hand to her chest. "I wasn't expecting anyone to be in here. You gave me quite a start."

Heather exhaled sharply. "I was going to go home when, well … I, well…"

"Don't worry, Heather dear. I'm sorry to disturb you. I think I left my glasses here. When I got settled in the library, I think I might have dozed off, just for a minute or two. Then I didn't want any tea, so I thought I'd take up my reading as I'd planned. I am a muddle-head. Oh, look, there they are. I must have put them down when I was talking to Mary. What are you doing, lass, hanging around like piffy on a rock bun, as our old Dora used to say?"

Heather's puzzlement must have shown on her face.

Izzy explained, "Dora was our help at home, and then she stayed on after she retired. She was a right Lancashire biddy and often came out with local expressions like that."

"Ah, I see." Despite her resolve, Heather's eyes flicked towards the easel one more time before she started to make her escape.

"Been having a peep, have you?" Izzy nodded in the direction of the painting. "He was at it when we were here earlier, wasn't he?"

"Huh," Heather grunted. Did nothing get by this old lady?

"You could do worse, from the little I've heard and seen. Good-looking enough, and I gather he does well at home. I know you thought he was shifty, but everyone here thinks he's wonderful. I think you must have been mistaken before. Perhaps your views were influenced by other things?"

"Oh, I'm not interested in him," Heather said quickly. "I'm not sure I even *like* what I've seen." She gave a small smile to lighten her tone and disguise her confusion.

Izzy's eyebrows raised just a fraction. "I think I said to you earlier, 'it takes a long time to truly know another.' Don't be too quick to judge, and don't be frightened to go with your heart. Don't settle for second best. It's not always best to be safe. Believe me, I know."

Heather was desperate to ask Izzy more, but her hopes were dashed.

"Forgive me. I'm an interfering old woman. Anyway, isn't it time you went home? You said you were just off, and I must get back to my book. I'll see you tomorrow, dear."

As she cycled home, Heather's thoughts spun. Will's painting had been a surprise. He displayed great expertise. She had read many books about composition and colour, rules of proportions and perspective. She enjoyed painting, but she was nowhere near as good as him. Again, she thought about the girl in the portrait. She was incredibly attractive, and Heather found herself resenting the fact. She looked a bit young for Will. He must be in his mid-twenties, and she looked eighteen at the most.

In her mind's eye, she saw him standing at the easel, the blond hairs on his brown arms extending to the backs of his hands. He held the brush in fine, long fingers. Very different to Brian's square-ended, practical fingers. Why was she making that comparison? *Get a grip, my girl*, she chastised herself as she got off her bike, unlatching the little gate and manoeuvring her bike up the front path.

CHAPTER 10

Berlin, 1927

Izzy could not believe she was being dragged back to England just when things were getting so interesting. However, Father's money would cease to arrive if she disobeyed, and staying was simply not an option. She plonked down onto the edge of the bed and huffed to herself, "It's so unfair. Delphi always gets what she wants, even now, from the other side of the world." Then she stood and moved to the window, gazing down at the garden. Summer was nearly done. Wind rocked the trees and damp leaves clung to the grass. Russet-coloured flowers bloomed but would soon be dropping their petals before frost and snow arrived. It all suited her gloomy mood.

Then she thought back to her trip to the cinema with Garrit and her spirit lightened, the frown leaving her face. She raised her shoulders, hugged herself, turned and smiled at her reflection in the mirror of the dressing table.

The cinema was very new and built in the Gothic style. It could seat well over a thousand people, and as Izzy had entered with Garrit she'd looked around and was amazed at the size and splendour. The film they had seen was so romantic but desperately sad. Still, the pogroms it was about, happened thirty years ago and more, and the film itself was quite old now.Surely things like that could no longer happen and even if attitudes were mixed they must be changing.

As they had emerged from the cinema, Izzy was in a thoughtful mood. The young Russian was so very handsome and brooding in his soldiers' uniform, while the Jewish girl he loved was young and pretty with her dark hair and eyes. The lovers were doomed, however, by the divide of their idealistic backgrounds and surroundings. When the heroine was banished from her home and all that was familiar, it made Izzy's eyes water. The conditions in the compound in which she was forced to live were so degrading and inhumane that Izzy was filled with anger on the young girl's behalf. Their house was damp; the plaster was blackened. She developed a cough, and her mother couldn't find any medicine for her daughter. The Russian was forced by his circumstances and beliefs to take part in her expulsion, but he managed to smuggle the girl some food. It ended with the strong implication that the girl would die, and he would be bereft and guilty.

When, in the dark, Garrit's hand had brushed hers on the armrest, Izzy had thought she would pass out. The film was already making her heart pound. She didn't move her hand away and left it for several moments before she risked a glance sideways. The moment she did, he turned his head and gazed at her, his sad eyes penetrating hers and making her want to throw her arms around him to give him comfort. But she didn't, though her heart raced. Surely, he must hear it.

She sniffed and blinked as they entered the foyer and hoped no one could see how pink her eyes were. Slowly and silently, they made their way to the heavy glass door. She was acutely aware of his hand under her elbow, guiding her through the crush. Instinctively she leaned into him, and when he looked down at her she gave him a small smile.

"Come, let's find a café and cheer ourselves up. I'm sorry if the film has upset you." Garrit took hold of her hand.

"I'm pleased you took me to see it," Izzy said. "I understand now, how hard it has been for your ancestors."

"And it still is in some places. Even here in Berlin, we are not always liked and sometimes I fear for the future."

"But how is that?" Izzy was genuinely puzzled.

"Only last week someone daubed an obscenity in paint on our neighbour's door. It said, '*Juden halte die Klappe und raus*', only it was not so polite."

"Get out? Get out of where?"

"Of Germany, I imagine," Garrit said.

"Oh, but that's awful."

"We learn to be careful. We don't raise our profile too much. Keep our heads down, so to speak."

"But your father's a doctor. He must surely be respected and liked."

Garrit shrugged but said nothing more on the subject, because at that moment it started to rain. He pulled Izzy into a small doorway, affording them a degree of shelter. She breathed deeply as the smell of his cologne overtook that of the tobacco emanating from the shop, and she was acutely aware of the warmth of his arm around her shoulders as he pulled her towards him and away from the rain. In a city such as Berlin, where anything was possible, she desperately wanted him to kiss her, to feel the heat of his lips on hers. Would they be dry and hard, or soft and sensitive?

She looked up at him and smiled.

"You are a very special person," he whispered.

She was sure he was about to bend his face to hers. Her core fluttered and swooped. Then his lips found her hairline, and the moment passed. Oh, why was he such a gentleman? But then she thought of Delphi and the cause of her banishment to Australia. Izzy sighed quietly into the fabric of Garrit's jacket.

"He's so handsome." Izzy was lying on her bed after reminiscing about her date with Garrit.

Gisela had returned to the bedroom and was sitting at the dressing table. She licked her finger and stroked her eyebrow, muttering as she did so, "Mmm, a bit too dark for my taste."

"What do you mean?"

"Jewish blood. Be careful, Izzy. You're so innocent sometimes. Those people are not always what they seem."

Izzy sat up and stared at her friend's back. "Explain, then I shan't be so innocent."

"I'm only saying…"

"Yes?"

"Well … they can't always be trusted." She turned to face Izzy. "They're not like us. I mean, they have peculiar habits and, well… They're not to be trusted," she repeated and shrugged her shoulders. "Just don't get too close. Papa certainly wouldn't like it."

Izzy swung her legs off the bed, stood and busied herself with looking in her bedside drawer to disguise her anger with Gisela. She hadn't thought much about it before but now she did, and she remembered other remarks and looks she had witnessed.

"You have no need to worry. I'm returning home next week, aren't I?"

"Right. Are you coming down?" Gisela bounced up and hurried to the door. "Dinner will be ready."

"I'll follow you in a minute. I'm not quite ready."

When Gisela left, Izzy sat down again on the edge of the bed. Her brain buzzed with guilt. She should have argued with Gisela and she hadn't. Her elbows rested on her knees, and her head sank onto her hands. She had skimmed an article only recently about anti-Jewish events becoming frequent but had not paid enough attention. In fact, in the last few months she hadn't read nearly as much as she used to. She had been having too much fun giddying around with Gisela's set.

Later in the week, Izzy managed to procure a newspaper. She had made the pretence of wanting to pop out and buy something for her return journey to England, but she had waited until Gisela was otherwise occupied.

"If you wait half an hour, I'll accompany you," Gisela had said.

"No, I shan't be long. It would be boring for you, anyway. I want something small for my niece to welcome her when she and Delphi return. I'll see you later."

Izzy hurriedly regarded all the transport toys available in the store. There seemed to be a plethora of those, but hardly anything suitable for a young girl. In haste, she found a little doll with a soft body and an endearing china face. Her pretty dress was sprigged with pink rosebuds. She had no idea if a child brought up in the Australian outback would have an interest in dolls. It would have to do.

She purchased the newspaper she was seeking. She also found a new paper published by Herr Goebbels, entitled *Der Angriff*.

The paper seller gave her a very odd look as she handed over her coins, so she quickly added a copy of *Jugend*, which had a glamorous image of a lady and a butterfly on the front cover and promised articles on Art Nouveau sensibilities. She shoved them all into her bag and hurried home. It wasn't until later in the afternoon, when Gisela was engaged in a music lesson, that Izzy had the opportunity to read what she had bought.

Der Angriff fully justified its name, with several articles written in rude and aggressive language and supporting its motto 'for the oppressed against the exploiters'. It was full of antisemitism and anti-parliamentarism. Goebbels had become *Gauleiter* of the Nazi Party in Berlin last year. Still, this newspaper had a very small circulation according to what it said in a tiny statement inside, despite the way it announced that information.

It can't pose much of a threat, despite the tone of it, Izzy thought.

In the main newspaper there was an interesting article about a new film, though. The article told of a man called Adolf Hitler, who had been at the Nuremberg rally of the Nazi Party earlier in the month. This man had greeted delegations from areas of Germany that were isolated and cut off from the Reich, like the Ruhr. He told them the 'foreigners' would be expelled, and the German people reunited. Many of the other gatherings he had organised had been in parks, and it seemed as if people had travelled on trains and in trucks or on foot to listen to this man and watch the film, *Eine Symphonie des Kampwillens*, he'd had made for the rally.

Mmm. A Symphony of the Will to Fight. *It sounds very militaristic in tone*, Izzy thought to herself.

At that point, Gisela called to her to come for supper. With haste, Izzy folded the two newspapers and stuffed them into her drawer, pulling some clothing over the top to conceal them.

CHAPTER 11

England, 1927

Izzy was disconsolate at being back in England. She hadn't seen Garrit for a last goodbye, but perhaps that was just as well. She had written him a long letter, but it didn't convey her innermost feelings. She wasn't sure of them herself.

Now she was in Manchester again, at the train station, but this time with her father, awaiting the arrival of her sister Delphi and her ten-year-old niece, Flora. She gazed in awe at the imposing square building with its large clock in the middle of the parapet. No flag flew today. The silhouette of the empty pole was black against the grey sky.

"I remember bringing your sister Rose here when she was going to Oxford for the first time. So much has changed in the last few years. We came by coach. Now look at all these motor cars," Papa said. "Your brother is gone, your mother too. Rose is in the sanatorium. Delphi has a daughter. I'm so pleased to have you here with me, child." He patted her arm, linked through his own.

They headed for the main entrance where Izzy was overcome by a trembling inside. It was a mix of excitement and nervous anticipation of seeing her sister again after all these years. Some people were standing waiting, some hurrying along. Porters with huge trolleys loaded with cases struggled through the throng; others answered queries, pointing or gesticulating. The sound of announcements of train times echoed around the hall. Pervading everything was the smell of coal, steam and creosote from the tracks. It seemed to be all noise and dust. There was a stiff breeze blowing from the direction of the platforms, and an enormous engine was clanking into sight, pulling carriages in the colours of the London, Midland and Scottish Railway Company. It screeched to a halt. A belch of steam and a strong smell was produced. Izzy covered her nose with her scarf, as did others.

Looking up, there were the great wrought-iron trusses of the roof and the cast-iron struts and girders. Her father's words returned from across the years; he had explained it all to her on her first visit to this place of extraordinary achievement when she was a little girl. "The London and North East Railway Company added six new platforms since the turn of the century," he had said. "This is your future Izzy, my child. We can be so proud of our country and its achievements. I remember saying the same to Rose."

Izzy thought about all that had happened since then. The Great War to end them all, her eldest sister opening a school … and Delphi going to Australia in disgrace, and now returning with the source of that shame — her child born out of wedlock because her lover had been killed. Would she have married George? Izzy supposed so, but nothing was certain in this life. And now she was here, when her own life in Berlin had held so much promise. Would she ever see Garrit again? He would surely meet somebody else, despite what he had whispered to her following that glorious visit to the cinema, 'You are a very special person.'

Like in a film, the steam from the trains suddenly cleared, and Delphi stood holding the hand of a pretty, dark-haired child. To Izzy, her sister looked the same as she had on the day she had departed — still slim and so beautiful. Her hat was less stylish, and her clothes seemed old-fashioned, but she still turned heads as she stepped forwards. The child looked up with a worried expression, and Delphi bent her head to catch the words, saying something that apparently eased the child's anxiety because a small smile played around her little face. Izzy saw her sister's expression change as she spotted her father. Was that fleeting anxiety? Surely not. Delphi laughed in the face of fear.

She arrived through the barrier and came skipping towards them, still light as a wisp of smoke. Her child followed on with the porter and all their cases.

Papa kissed Delphi on each cheek and said, "Welcome home." He sounded stiff to Izzy's ears, but her sister thanked him easily enough. Then she stepped forward and hugged Izzy.

"You haven't been back long from Germany, I gather," she said.

"No." What more could she say?

Papa leaped in. "But she was happy to come home to see you, weren't you, Izzy? After all, you were there some time. I'm sure your wider education was complete. And you wanted to see Rose, of course."

"Yes." *Little walls of lies we build around ourselves*, Izzy thought. *All in the name of protection.*

"Flora, this is your Grandpapa and your Aunt Izzy." The child held out her hand in a sad formal little gesture that she had learned somewhere. The anxious expression had returned.

Izzy took it, but with her other hand around the child's slim shoulder she pulled her close and kissed the top of her head. "Hello, Flora. I've been so looking forward to meeting you," she said.

"Have you?" Flora answered, sounding surprised.

"Yes, and I have a little gift for you back at the house. It came with me all the way from Germany." She was rewarded by the child's sweet smile.

"You'll grow to love it here as I do, I promise," Delphi said, looking down at her daughter. "I was so happy here when I was a child. There is such a lot to show you. I'm truly pleased to be here with you all." Delphi took hold of Izzy's hand and gave it a little squeeze. "You have changed so much, little sister. You were a child when I left and now you are a woman, and a beauty too. You have Rose's fine hair, and you have my colouring, but your face is all your own, elfin and pretty. And how is Rose? I gather, from your telegraph, that she is much better."

"Yes, such a relief. Soon you will see for yourself."

Outside the train station, Delphi climbed into her father's car, followed by Flora and then Izzy. "We'll go home," her father said. "Get you settled in."

Izzy fought to find something to say. She was resentful, but she had to squash that down and be happy that her sister was here. Her little niece seemed a sweetie. Quiet, but that wasn't surprising. She must be tired, and it was all strange to her.

"As for Dora…" Papa continued, seemingly unaware of the turmoil concerning the relationship between his daughters, "she has hardly been able to contain her impatience. She stays in her room for most of the time these days and copes with the mending and suchlike. I think she enjoys the peace, but if she ventures down to the kitchen she tends to interfere with things and the new maid, Betty, gets quite short with her. You've had to sort out more than one row, haven't you, Izzy?"

"Yes, Papa." Izzy saw her father frown in the rear-view mirror. She must try and be more gracious.

"I miss Grandma and Pops," Flora was whispering to her mother, but Izzy still heard what she said and caught the plaintive expression on her little face.

"I know, darling, but we couldn't stay, could we? After Pops died, Grandma needed Aunt Margaret, didn't she? She needed to move, and we couldn't manage on our own. Anyway, you said you wanted to meet your English family."

"Mmm. It'll be a *grand* adventure." A cheeky smile appeared, and her voice rose.

"Yes, indeed, you little minx." Delphi smiled at her and Izzy caught a sparkle in the child's expression that was identical to the one her mother had had when they were growing up.

"It's a big change for all of you, then," Izzy ventured. "Perhaps it will be for longer than a holiday visit."

"Well, yes. We couldn't have managed all the hands and the finances on our own, though, and my mother-in-law was looking forward to moving to the city to be with her daughter and other grandchildren."

"I'm sure she'll miss you both," Izzy said charitably.

"In some ways, maybe not in others."

Izzy caught a tiny flicker of desolation, and felt the beginnings of compassion for Delphi. Her life must have been far from easy on the other side of the world, among comparative strangers.

"So, how was that long voyage?" Izzy's papa stretched his neck to see the child in his driving mirror.

"It was fine, thank you. Rainier lent me some books and we played deck games. I didn't like the storms, though."

"She was very seasick, I'm afraid, weren't you?" Delphi turned to her daughter.

"And who is Rainier?"

"He was a very nice friend on the ship," Flora answered.

"Was he your age?" Mr Strong asked.

Flora giggled. "Oh no. He was Mummy's friend."

Papa looked back at Delphi. "Oh, I see," he said. Delphi could not hold his gaze.

One minute Izzy was sympathetic to this quixotic sister, and the next she wasn't sure at all. Delphi was always one to attract attention, so she shouldn't have been too surprised that she'd met someone on the ship. It was a long voyage.

Izzy tried not to stare at her sister, but Delphi had turned her head and was gazing out of the opposite window.

CHAPTER 12

Yorkshire, 1975

Heather waited for Brian's knock at the front door.

"Will you be out late?" June was ironing. "It makes no difference, but I was planning to pop round and see Deirdre. She's got some photos of her new granddaughter back from the chemist. You might need to take a key in case you get back before I do."

"I'll take a key. Not sure what we're doing, although Brian mentioned a film. He'll have a plan, I'm sure, but there's no way I want to see that thing about the shark."

"*Jaws?* No, I wouldn't fancy that. I think the other one was *Monty Python and the Holy Grail.*"

"Can't see that being his cup of tea either, although it sounds like a good laugh."

"Maybe just stay in, then. I'll be gone in the next half hour, so you can have the front room to yourselves." Heather's mum gave an exaggerated wink.

"Mu-um!"

Ten minutes later, June was shrugging into her jacket.

"You don't need to be in such a hurry," Heather said.

"Who, me? I'm anxious to see all those photos." She laughed. When she opened the front door, Brian was closing the gate with precise care. "Hello, Brian, love. I'm off out. Have a nice evening, the two of you."

Brian stepped over the threshold and gave Heather a peck on the cheek as she stood back to let him in. "I checked out the pictures," he said, "but I decided there wasn't anything on that we would enjoy."

Although Heather knew this to be true, she was annoyed at his presumption on her behalf. "Let's go for a walk then. It's a lovely evening."

As they strolled, hand in hand, Brian started to tell Heather about his day. She half-listened and nodded and made non-committal sounds at what she presumed were the right moments. Her mind was elsewhere — on that painting, that young and very attractive girl with the green eyes and startling hair. Who was she? Then she mentally shook herself and looked up at Brian, who was finishing a story about some client or other.

They entered the park and Brian guided her to a bench. As they sat he put his arm around her shoulders, but she didn't lean into him. There was no one about and the huge rhododendron bushes shielded them from intrusive eyes. Heather casually thought it was a shame that all the showy purple flowers had finished and only the spikey stamens among the leathery leaves were left.

"Did you know that every part of the rhododendron is poisonous? Even honey made from the flowers isn't supposed to be good for you," Brian said.

"Really? How sad. You know so many things, Brian."

"Yes, well, I read a lot."

"Do you know about badgers?"

"Badgers? Where on earth did that spring from? I know they are dirty wild things that carry disease. Something to do with TB. Stop talking and kiss me."

He pressed her shoulder so that she leaned into him and automatically turned her head to receive his lips. Her mind was elsewhere, but gradually her attention turned to him. His kiss became more ardent and his other hand came to rest on her right breast. She placed her hand on his cheek, which encouraged him to move his hand down and then up under her jumper.

She pulled away. "Not here, Brian. It's a bit public."

"No one comes this way at this time in the evening. The children are long gone, and the dog walkers will be on the main path." He leaned in again and his hand found her nipple under her clothing. "Oh, Heather," he moaned. "Let's go home. Your mother won't be back yet." He stood before she could answer. Taking hold of her hands, he pulled her to her feet. "Come on."

She followed but realised her own reluctance. They'd had a hurried flounder at his house last week, but it hadn't been very satisfying for her. She'd been happy enough to go to bed with him. After all, they'd been together for a while; he was kind and gentle and she really liked him, but it had all seemed quick. Perhaps he'd been nervous, she'd reasoned. Maybe he wasn't as experienced as she'd assumed. Neither was she. He'd wanted her to get dressed straight after, and he'd spoken of having to meet his brother for something or other. There'd been no languid afterglow. It had all been a bit clinical and unromantic.

Now, his arm around her shoulders was warm, and as she fell into step next to him, he said, "Heather, I really like you. You know that, don't you?" His speed increased.

Alarm bells began to ring. Izzy's words flew around Heather's head. *Don't settle for second best.*

As she turned her key and pushed open the front door, Heather heard a clatter in the kitchen. The relief was enormous. Her mother had returned early.

"Mum's home. Sorry, Brian. You'd better go."

"Really?"

"I'm not doing anything now. Not here, when she's downstairs."

"When will I see you? It must be soon. I need you."

"I'll call."

"Oh, alright then," he huffed.

She felt guilty but was glad to watch him leave.

"Has Brian gone?" asked June, emerging from the kitchen.

"Yes, he had to go." *Gone home to give himself one*, she thought. "Oh, Mum! It's not going to work out. He's simply not the one."

"You must follow your heart, but a little bit of head helps, too. I followed my heart totally, even though I knew things could be better, and look what happened there."

"I know Dad left, but you've never really told me much, Mum."

"Sit down, darling. Let's have a chat." June pulled a chair out from the table.

"Let's have a glass of wine," Heather said.

Once they were settled, Heather shifted on her seat and waited, avoiding looking at her parent.

"Before we married, he was loving. Later, I was often taken for granted, or so it seemed to me. I never accused him of it, though. We didn't talk because I feared an argument. Not that he was ever physical. No, never that." She twirled the stem of her wine glass as she contemplated. "It was partly my fault for allowing things to pass without challenge. He was always controlling, in a mild sort of way. I didn't realise it until I could look at things more dispassionately. He both intrigued and wounded me. If we did argue, it was me who was penitent even if he had done something outrageous. Then I'd buzz around him, trying to make things right when probably I should have left him to stew."

"So, you still partly blame yourself?"

"It takes two, doesn't it? But yes, I suppose I do."

"Mmm. But if he was controlling in a mental sort of way, that's not right. You shouldn't have let him, Mum."

"I thought I was doing right by you." A frown appeared on Heather's forehead. "Oh, I don't mean it's your fault. Not at all. Don't ever think that. I thought if I kept things together by caving in, kept the peace, so to speak, it would be better for you. I didn't want you to hear rowing all the time."

"He controlled me too, though. It was his way."

"Yes. I think it's made you very underconfident, love. I'm responsible for that as well."

Heather sat, saying nothing more as she tried to straighten out her thoughts and emotions.

As she lay in bed that night, she was becoming more certain that Brian was not the man for her and that if history was to stop repeating itself, she must tell him so. Perhaps it was better to build a wall and have nothing more to do with men. She couldn't seem to get it right.

At that moment between wakefulness and sleep, she suddenly wondered what had happened to Izzy. Surely Garrit could have been her one true love, but had she ever seen him again?

CHAPTER 13

England, 1927

The next time Izzy visited Rose at the sanitorium, Delphi accompanied her. Flora was helping Dora make some jam tarts. When they left her, she had flour on her cheek and a wide smile.

"See you later, little chook," Delphi said, and Flora giggled.

"Cheep, cheep," she replied and flapped her bent elbows like fledgling wings.

As they left the house and headed for the omnibus stop, Delphi said, "When I went with Papa last time, Rose looked very pale. Doctor Brown said she was out of danger, though. I can't tell you how relieved I am."

Yes, because if she had died, you'd never have made amends for the grief you caused. Izzy tried to put a stop to those thoughts. They were beneath her dignity and uncalled for. Delphi had matured, though Izzy still found it hard to appreciate this. Her sister had admitted her true and enduring love for George, Flora's father; it had not diminished during all her years in Australia. And now she had met Rainier, a French vineyard owner, on the ship back to England. She had been open about her desperate sadness at saying goodbye to him when he'd had to leave the ship at St Nazaire to return to his own home. She doubted they would meet again.

It seemed that the Strong sisters needed to be true to their name. Izzy doubted she would meet anyone as fascinating and charismatic as Garrit. Not even Dr Benjamin Brown held her interest as much, though he was clearly an admirer.

She had spoken with him several times, mainly about Rose's condition and progress. But he would probably prefer Delphi now. Everyone did. That was fine. Izzy wasn't looking for another love. Not when Garrit still occupied most of her waking thoughts.

Together, Izzy and Delphi climbed the steps up to the large and heavy-looking door. There was a bell-pull to one side, which Izzy tugged twice. The door opened, and a nurse in a white uniform with an old-fashioned white headdress smiled at them. She looked more like a nun from the last century than a modern nurse.

"Miss Strong, ma'am." She nodded at Izzy and stood back to let them in. "Mrs Redfern is sitting in the conservatory today. She had a good night. Would you like me to accompany you?"

"Thank you. This is Rose's sister, Mrs Dight. She's come all the way from Australia."

"I do believe my colleague said you visited once before. My goodness, Mrs Dight, that is a long way. Your sister will be ever so pleased to see you again, I'm sure."

Delphi simply smiled and nodded. Izzy wondered about the truth of that. Rose had said nothing about her sister's arrival, and there had been no obvious animosity, but Izzy knew that the row between them had been terrible.

The corridors were long and painted like any other hospital: duck-egg blue below the dark green dado and cream above.

The odd picture here or there might help, Izzy thought.

Doors with glass panes which were covered by curtains on the other side led off the corridor, but every so often there were windows through which Izzy could see small sitting rooms with high-backed chairs and occasional tables. A few patients appeared to be dozing or reading.

"May we speak to a doctor before we go to see my sister?" Izzy glanced at Delphi. "Mrs Dight here would really like to know first-hand how she is progressing and what treatment is being administered. Last time she visited, my father spoke to the doctor."

"Of course, Miss Strong. Perhaps you would like to sit in here. It's specifically for visitors rather than patients." The nurse opened a door and ushered them into a small room, sparsely but comfortably furnished.

"The condition is very dangerous, Delphi. There is a strict protocol here about visitors and patients being kept separate when patients are contagious," Izzy explained.

"I know so little. I feel a bit helpless," Delphi said.

"It was a long time before Rose was permitted any visitors," said Izzy. "Michael was beside himself with worry but fortunately, by some miracle, he hasn't caught it. The school was quarantined for quite a while, though. Things have been very, very difficult."

Delphi sat and fidgeted with her cuffs. Then she stood and paced before sitting again. The door opened and the doctor entered. Izzy thought his smile aimed at being encouraging, and she glanced at her sister to see how she would react.

"Miss Strong and ... Mrs Dight?"

"Yes, I'm Rose's other sister," said Delphi.

Dr Brown shook her hand and then Izzy's. A smile lit his face as he caught Izzy's eye. "It's good to meet you," he said, turning back to Delphi. "Your sister is making steady progress."

"I know it's a killer, this disease. Will she survive?"

"I am confident now that your sister will live. It was not like that at first, though, and she will always have a weakness of the lungs. She must be careful not to get over-tired in the future, and any colds and coughs will have to be monitored carefully."

"What treatment does she have?"

"Plenty of fresh air now. We had to collapse her lung to rest it at first. There is little else we can do. She's very lucky indeed."

"I thought there was some sort of injection?"

"No. In France, experiments continue and there seems to have been some success with a vaccination to prevent one from catching the disease, but I'm afraid we are nowhere near a medical cure yet," Dr Brown explained.

"I see," Delphi sighed.

"Take heart, Mrs Dight. Your sister is getting better. It's been a long process, but she is one of the lucky ones. Would you like to come now? I know Rose is looking forward to seeing you. She has spoken of you a lot, and I can see why now."

As I suspected, Izzy thought. *She still has the power to charm everyone she meets.*

"Delphi, Mrs Dight, will go to see Rose on her own first," Izzy said. "They still have much to discuss. Perhaps I might wait here before I join them."

"That would be perfect," said Dr Brown. "While you wait, may I have a word, Miss Strong?"

Izzy's anxiety bubbled over. "My sister Rose is all right, isn't she?"

"Yes, yes, indeed. This is another matter entirely. I'll return shortly."

Dr Brown left the room to lead Delphi to Rose. Izzy was restless. What on earth could be his business with her? She stood and paced, looking at the heavy wooden chairs and the beige walls. The dark velvet curtains and the aspidistra on the window ledge made the room feel gloomy and oppressive.

Izzy had her back to the door as it opened, and she turned around, thoroughly startled. Dr Brown was back. Her heart began to thump in anticipation of bad news, although she didn't dare imagine what that could be.

"Dr Brown, you have me worried." She tried to smile but was sure it looked more like a grimace.

"Miss Strong, please don't be anxious." The doctor smiled. "This is a personal matter and nothing to do with your sister's health and progress." He paused. "We have met several times, and each time you have impressed me with your good sense and level-headedness."

Goodness, he sounds formal. And not a little pompous, Izzy thought. *His dark eyes remind me of Garrit, but they have none of his sparkle.* She began to feel wistful, but managed to snap back to the present.

"I was hoping you might like to accompany me to a performance in Manchester one night soon."

"Oh, I see. Is that at the Palace Theatre?"

"My goodness me, no. They have a flapper show. Not appropriate at all, I think." He smiled again.

Izzy thought The Palace sounded a great wheeze, but said nothing.

Dr Brown, Benjamin, continued, "No, this is at the Royal Opera House. I read that in Covent Garden in London there is to be the very first performance in this country of Puccini's posthumous opera *Turandot*. They say it is to be the equal of *La Bohème*. I should love to take you there. This will be a far more modest performance but still good, I'm sure. I know you would enjoy it."

I wonder how he knows that, Izzy thought. "I'm sure it would be delightful," she said out of politeness.

Dr Brown immediately took this as her assent which, in retrospect, she supposed it was.

She could see an outline of a string vest through the fabric of his cream shirt. His brown tie and tweed suit were smart, but very conservative. His hair was slicked down with Brylcreem and his face was pleasant, but Izzy was sure that his thick moustache would not be agreeable if he kissed her. Oh, well, he had given his earnest invitation charmingly enough, and he did have delightfully dark eyes.

CHAPTER 14

Yorkshire, 1975

Izzy and Heather were sitting in the library. For the past hour, Izzy had been continuing her story. She looked up from her lap at Heather's intense expression.

"So, you see, my dear, I did meet someone else. Benjamin Brown was a charming escort, and he certainly knew a lot about the classics — from his education as a doctor, I imagine."

"Oh, Izzy," said Heather. "Did you have an enchanting evening? Fancy! The Royal Opera House sounds so grand. Did you go out with him again? Did you ever see Garrit again, though? Did you go back to Berlin?"

"That's enough for today," Izzy said. "I thought I might pop along to the craft room and see Mary. I've also met a lovely gentleman named Emile. He lived in France for a while, and he said we have been expats in common. That's the word, isn't it? I was only a visitor abroad, though. I didn't live in Berlin permanently, and I didn't work there. Anyway, I digress. I have *das Stelldichen* or, as Emile would say, a *rendezvous*." A small smile played at the corners of her mouth, and her eyes danced as Heather raised her eyebrows questioningly. Izzy laughed. "You are a romantic at heart. I'm too old for all that, but you are not. Come with me, and we'll see if Will is painting at this hour again." She winked at Heather and seemed to take delight in her confusion.

Once upstairs, Heather pushed open the craft room door for Izzy and turned to leave.

"No, after you, dear girl. Come on. I had you down as being brave. Don't tell me you are not," Izzy said.

Heather was not. She knew she wasn't. She'd had years of being told she wasn't good enough. Her father had always expected more. Her exam results had never been enough, no matter how impressive they were. When she'd taken part in a swimming competition, her father had said she should have gone faster and won the race instead of coming second, even though she had beaten many to get to the final. As a Brownie, she'd been told she could have collected more badges and won the shield that someone else had taken home.

Heather took a deep breath and muttered, "You're a mischief-maker."

Izzy gave a soft chortle and made a beeline for Mary. She was speaking to a grey-haired gentleman with a bushy moustache who Heather took to be Emile. She thought he must remind Izzy of Dr Benjamin Brown. He had an Airfix model of an aeroplane, half-made, in front of him.

Heather looked around, wondering what to do next, but quickly realised there was no sign of Will here. She was unsure if she was relieved or disappointed. There was a gentle buzz of conversation. Several ladies were sitting together, nattering over their knitting. The easel still stood in the corner. This time there was no cloth covering it, but Heather could only see the back of the canvas. It was tempting. She could approach and have a casual glance at the image to see if it had progressed. She faltered, undecided. Will's paints were strewn on the table in careless fashion, and a palette with some blobs of colour lay next to them. The brushes, though, were clean and lined up, with others lying in a cylinder placed across the bottom ledge of the easel.

Heather found herself comparing this to the way Brian would have organised his tubes of oils, should he ever take up anything so creative. She decided they would be carefully arranged by colour, but then he could never be that imaginative. He preferred stamps and researching the history of his finds. She had been invited to come and see his collection, and had spent the time surreptitiously glancing around his room. It had been so tidy and had told her little about him that she didn't already know. A pair of slippers had been placed neatly together against the wall. There had been no clothes left in a heap. His bed had been pristine, without a single wrinkle.

Drifting back from the memory, Heather looked again at Will's paints. No, Brian could never be this imaginative. He would never be so fanciful, so mysterious, so extravagant. He could never be romantic enough to paint his lover. He would always look for the perfect partner and never the perfect love.

She visualised the portrait. The girl's eyes had stared back at her, full of love. Will had created that love.

Heather turned and hurried from the room.

The next time Heather saw Brian, she knew what she had to do. It wouldn't be easy. She was usually on the receiving end of such conversations, so she knew how they went. Except with Kev, of course, when her humiliation at his infidelity had come after office hours one evening. Working late to finish a rush task, she had discovered him in the worst of compromising positions across the boardroom table with Tracey, the accounts manager.

"Shall we go to our usual place and grab a swift half?" Brian said when he arrived at seven o'clock, on the dot.

"Come in, Brian. Perhaps I could have a word." Heather had primed her mum to keep well out of the way while she talked to him. She led Brian into the front room and closed the door behind them, but she didn't sit down.

"What's going on?" Brian asked. He'd been about to take a seat, but now remained standing in the middle of the room.

"Brian." She cleared her throat. "I'm so sorry. This isn't working for me. There's no one else, but I need to call it a day."

"I beg your pardon? What on earth are you saying? Are you ditching me? After everything I've done for you?"

Heather was tempted to pick up on that one. She wasn't sure to what Brian referred, but she decided to leave him his view of himself. She fully understood what this sort of conversation could do to one's self-esteem. "You've been very kind," she said, aware of sounding feeble.

"Kind?"

Oh Lord, please let this be over, she thought. "I need more time to decide what I want for my life."

"Claptrap. Leftist rubbish."

"Brian, it's over." She was getting irate now, and only just managing to hide it.

"Got someone else in mind, have you? Someone else like the famous Kev, about whom I've heard so often, is it? Someone more with it; someone trendier. Much good may it do you."

I most certainly have not mentioned him more than once, she thought, but she let it go, not wishing to prolong this. "There's no one else. I said."

"I'll be off, then. Good luck to you." His sarcasm was not lost on her and she stood still as he stormed from the room. She heard the front door slam but couldn't turn to the window to watch him march down the front path.

She stayed there for several moments, and then the door to the room pushed open and June poked her head round. Seeing Heather alone, she came in.

"That's it, then. Well done." She spread her arms and Heather took refuge. Grown up as she was, she wasn't too old to appreciate the smell, warmth and familiarity of her mum.

"Oh, Mum, that was awful."

"But it's done now, and you'll move on."

Heather saw Izzy a couple of days later.

"You look a bit peaky," said Izzy. "Are you all right?"

"I didn't sleep too well."

"At your age? That's for older people like me. Something on your mind?"

Heather heaved a sigh. "I finished with Brian, my boyfriend. He didn't take it too well, and I understand how he feels. It's the pits, I know. It's happened to me more than once."

"I told you before. If it's not right for you, it's not. You can't live your life in safe mode without love, but it is possible to be loved and be safe. I missed my opportunity of love by being too safe. More than once, but especially in Berlin. Don't you do the same."

"What of Dr Benjamin Brown?" asked Heather.

"Ah, yes, well, he was a safe one. Very knowledgeable, polite, a good host, caring ... boring." Izzy smiled at the memory. "Like you and your Brian. He took care of me, but he had no imagination."

"That sounds exactly like Brian," Heather said, beginning to perk up.

"Benjamin Brown was a charming distraction but ultimately too dull and precise. I finished my friendship with him before it had gone too far, much to the chagrin of Papa."

"Oh?"

"He had seen a comfortable, professional man who would take care of us both. Papa was getting old by that time." Her eyes glazed. "Benjamin reminded me a little of Garrit, with his dark eyes and black hair. Not the moustache, though." She gave a young girl's giggle. "I had tried to kid myself that he might be a good match. But he didn't stir me like Garrit did."

"Did you go back to Berlin?"

"Oh yes, many times. And Garrit came here. We were close but…" She shrugged. "It's not for me to tell you what to do, but think on what I said just now, my dear. Don't settle for safe, and don't build walls around yourself either."

CHAPTER 15

Berlin, 1934

Izzy visited Berlin two or three times after she'd returned to England, but only for a couple of weeks at a time. Her Papa needed her. When Rose had recovered sufficiently to return to the school, her life there with Michael was demanding, and Izzy was obliged to help there, too. Delphi had gone to live in France as Mrs Rainier Harman, and she and Flora seemed very happy. There was only Izzy left to look after her father. She understood her role and accepted it.

She had maintained a correspondence with one or two people in Germany and had friends with whom she could stay when she made a short visit. Garrit and she had met, walked together, been out for morning coffee, but that was all. Life was funny. They always just picked up where they had left off. They chatted and laughed together. Intimacy was limited to a few kisses, but he was in her heart and that made it impossible for her to look at anyone else.

Her latest visit to Berlin would be much longer. She expected to be there for almost two months. Everyone at home had encouraged her. She had earned it, but was still anxious about leaving them all. She had therefore made arrangements with servants and friends, who would let her know if there were any problems.

Her anticipation on the journey was tangible. She couldn't wait to return to the life she'd had back in 1927. She dreamed of lazy lunches, coffee at the Café König, and evening recitals. When she remembered outings with handsome army officers, she smiled. Then her thoughts turned to meeting Garrit again and her pulse raced. He had never married either. He supported his mother in looking after Ester and he continued to work at the Friedrich Wilhelm Universität. As far as she knew, anyway. They wrote to each other, sent cards at Christmas, but their friendship, while surviving, had not grown closer with her absence. Still, she felt a tingle of excitement at seeing him again.

There had been rumours of troubles among some of the population in Berlin, but Izzy wasn't sure how much to believe. She was just delighted to be there again, and was ready to partake of all the city had to offer.

Gisela had married an army officer back in 1929. This time, Izzy was staying with them in their smart house.

When she was met at the station, Gisela hugged her, welcomed her, and took her to the home she had made with Otto, her husband. Izzy was shown to her stylish guest bedroom.

"Come down as soon as you are unpacked, and we'll have a glass of something to celebrate your return. Otto will be here soon, I hope. I'm excited for you to meet him. I'm so proud of his rise. He's doing very well."

Izzy was full of eagerness too. This visit held so much promise. She had to try and see Garrit as soon as possible. "This room is beautiful," she said as she entered the *Wohnzimmer* and looked around at the furnishings, the paintings on the walls and the modern lamp in the corner, which cast a warm glow on the soft cushions of the chairs. In another corner stood a traditional *Kachelofen* covered in dark green tiles that looked heavy and out of place.

Gisela followed her gaze. "Isn't it beautiful? So traditional. We had it built by a master and it's perfect in the winter. Too hot in this season to have it lit, of course."

"I thought you would be very modern and have some Bauhaus influence. You used to like the aesthetics and functionality."

Gisela's glance flicked towards the open door. "No, no. Very un-German now, in this new age. It's degenerate, in fact," she said. "Otto would not have done so well if it was thought he had sympathy for that. We'll talk of it no more."

"Oh, I see," Izzy said, not seeing at all. She was puzzled at the tone of Gisela's voice as well as her words.

Gisela rang a small bell and a middle-aged lady trundled in, wearing traditional dirndl costume and looking faintly ridiculous, Izzy thought. Anyway, wasn't it more Austrian than German? The poor woman was clearly too hot, and the outfit looked impractical. Her tight, low-cut bodice and puffed sleeves didn't suit her, and her white tights and button shoes looked uncomfortable, but her apron was pristine and well-pressed.

"Wine, please, for our guest and myself." Gisela sounded more imperious than she used to.

The woman bobbed her head and scuttled off to fetch the refreshment.

"Otto will be home soon," Gisela said again, looking at the clock on the wall. "He has been very busy recently, but he said he would come home earlier tonight."

"I'm so sorry I couldn't come to your wedding. Things at home are … difficult, as I wrote at the time. What regiment is he in?"

Gisela's response surprised Izzy. "Not part of the army, I'm pleased to say. He might be sent anywhere, had that been the case. He was in the *Sturmabteilung*, but he made a smart move at the right time and now he's with the *Schutzstaffel*, and since the *SS-Gau Berlin* was formed we can live here. He got a promotion out of it too. He doesn't have to wear that awful brown shirt anymore. Much more handsome in black." She giggled like the old Gisela Izzy had known. "So much better and more respected where he is. Heinrich Himmler is *Reichsführer-SS* now, and it's all so much more suitable."

Izzy frowned, but Gisela took it for ignorance rather than disapproval.

She sighed and undertook to explain. "Three or four years ago, Otto helped provide protection for rallies and assemblies. Röhm had overall command for a while, but he got too big for his boots, by far. Some say he even plotted against Herr Hitler. It's been more structured and organised since he was executed but really, not such a pleasant unit. Some say they have become thuggish. Otto was involved at the beginning in some incidents with such stupid folk, when opposing parties disrupted all the valid work of our wonderful *Führer*. So many Communists. They are dangerous in the extreme." She seemed not to notice Izzy's quietness as she gushed on. "Otto wasn't actually with Hitler when the SS went with him to arrest Röhm. I was pleased. There was a lot of fighting." She leaned towards Izzy and lowered her voice. "He, Röhm, was one of *those*, you know, so what can you expect with such depravity?" Then she uttered the word in a shocked whisper: "Homosexual." She sat up and clapped her hands like a child, and Izzy was taken aback. "Oh, but you should have been here last January. We had such a celebration when Adolf won and took the position of *Reich Chancellor*. There was a torchlight procession to rival anywhere else you can imagine. Such a relief when things had slipped only the year before. Still, many of those wretched Jews fled. So many anti-Nazi organisations have gone, thank goodness. And now Herr Hitler is our *Führer*." She gave a self-satisfied smile and nodded.

Izzy was light-headed as her heart raced. Jews fleeing? She had heard about the unrest but had assumed that, now Adolf Hitler had got what he wanted, things would quieten down. "Do you see any of the old crowd?" she asked as innocently as she could, brushing imaginary fluff from her dress to avoid eye contact with Gisela.

"One or two. Be warned, though, Izzy. Things have changed, and for the better too. There have been such disruptive factions and the Jews are getting it all their own way, you know. There are some who we certainly have no wish to see again. Himmler's expanded the *Schutzstaffel* no end. Otto's in the *Allegemeine-SS*, so that branch tries to help sort out the racial problems we seem to have in Berlin, now. Honestly, Izzy, it is so changed. Something certainly needs to be done. Next month, Otto's going for a spell at this new *SS-Junkerschule*. It's for officer candidates. I'm so proud of him. He'll receive some first-rate training and information about the way things must go."

Izzy's thoughts were spinning. This all sounded so unlike the Gisela she had known before. They'd had fun, laughed together, flirted with all the boys and refused to take life too seriously. Now, Gisela sounded harsh and uncompromising. "But I thought the Jewish question was jogging along," said Izzy. "Don't they have their own churches, schools and so on and keep to themselves?"

"They seem to think they can have exactly what they want. They aren't short of a few Reichsmarks when so many of us are still struggling."

Izzy glanced around the room. *Struggling? Really?* she thought.

"Hitler is making Germany strong again," Gisela said. "If a few people lose some of their freedoms — which, by the way, are not serving the common good in any way — then so be it. They need to be put back in their place." She nodded. "When Otto was involved in the public book burning last year, it was for the good of a pure Germany. Izzy, you must understand, these Jews are not like us. That's why so many teachers and lawyers simply had to be sacked. We cannot afford for their ideas to spread. Now, where is that foolish woman with our wine?"

CHAPTER 16

Izzy was pleased with herself. She had told Gisela that she needed to do some shopping, but she had waited until she knew her hostess was engaged with one of her groups of women.

"We meet once each month, and I can't miss it. We discuss things relevant to us. Herr Hitler encourages our feminine charm. We do whatever we can to complement our menfolk. After all, Frau Goebbels said, 'if a German girl must choose between marriage and a career, she will always be encouraged to marry, because that is what is best for a woman.' She is correct, of course. We promote a strong Aryan society, and I cannot wait until I have children of my own. I am so disappointed that after five years, I am still not a mother. You could come too, as a visitor. I'm certain you would find it enriching."

"Er…" Izzy was caught off-guard. She had a very different afternoon planned. "Maybe next time. I'm not expected, and I have some errands to run in town."

"Yes, you're probably right. If Frau Engel isn't expecting you, it will alter all her arrangements and catering. Do say you'll come next time, though. If only I'd thought about it sooner. I'm such a *Trottel*." She blew out her cheeks and slapped her forehead. "*Dummkopf.* It would have been such an opportunity for you to see how well we are supporting our men here in Germany."

"Yes, indeed. I see that Germany has moved forwards in many ways since I was here last."

"We were penalised in a most vile and terrible way after the Great War. It caused much hardship. Now, thank goodness, we are on the track to unrivalled success. Your Great Britain could learn much from us."

As Izzy rode on the bus and watched out of the window, she saw large houses pass, followed by apartment blocks and then open spaces filled with rubble where building work was in progress. When she walked from the bus stop to the block where Garrit still lived with his family, she was shocked. The area seemed downcast. There were some properties with boarded windows and others that were evidently empty. Several shops had a yellow star on the door and in the window, which she had not seen before. On one of these windows, a black daub said: *The Jews are our misfortune. Don't buy here.* She must ask Garrit about that.

Despite all this, Izzy's anticipation could not be dampened as she approached Garrit's block of flats. As she glanced up, she saw his face at the window and waved. Before she had reached the door, he was there to greet her, out of breath but smiling. As he kissed her on each cheek, she was enchanted anew by his physique, his smell and his enthusiasm. As he pulled back, he took her by the shoulders and looked at her, his head on one side. His smile was infectious, and she grinned back at him.

"I'm so pleased to see you again," she said.

"And I you. Mother and Ester can't wait. Come on up." He took her hand and led her to the stairs. Halfway up, he turned. His eyes were dark and deep, piercing hers. He pulled her up level with him and kissed her gently on the lips. "I'm so pleased to see you again, *mein Schatz.*"

Am I really? she thought. *Am I truly your treasure? Ah, but where will this go?*

As on previous occasions, Ester sat in her chair. In front of her was a tray with puzzle pieces. She was managing to manipulate a chunky wooden piece into position as Izzy entered the room. She looked up and beamed. Izzy crossed the floor in three strides and flung her arms around the thin shoulders of the girl. "Ester, you have turned into a beautiful young woman. How lovely to be here with you again after so long."

"Izzy, thank you. I'm so pleased to see you, and so is Garrit." She glanced at her brother and grinned with mischief.

"Ester!" Garrit said, and he gave her shoulder a playful cuff.

"*Mutti*," she called. "Izzy is here. *Komm und sieh.*"

"I do see," Garrit's mother said as she hurried into the room, her arms outstretched. "Let me look at you." Echoing Garrit's stance, she took Izzy by the shoulders and stood back. "You are as lovely as ever. Sit, please." She indicated the best seat in the room.

The afternoon passed with gentle laughter and light-hearted chatter, but Izzy realised that this family had changed in subtle ways. They had all lost weight, Frau Shain looked older than her age and Garrit looked exhausted. Ester, apart from being older, was little different. Reading between the lines, Izzy gathered that they all protected her from much of the world. Garrit's father had lost his position with the reputable group of middle-class doctors with whom he had worked for many years. Now he worked in the poorer parts of the city, often being paid in food and sometimes not being paid at all.

Garrit still did a little translation work for the university, but it was unofficial and poorly paid. His position so lowly enough for him to continue to be useful to the Aryan professors and teachers, but in a quiet way.

After refreshment, Izzy and Garrit took a walk outside. Izzy remembered a previous time when the neat turf had been dotted with tiny spring flowers, and the air had been fresh and clean. Now the grass was long and spiky, and what flowers had strived to survive had disappeared into its midst.

"We have had a good life here in Berlin. All my people did well and prospered. We have been free to worship as we want and to hold respected positions, but now that is changing, and since last year it has become very difficult. It's really not so long ago that Rathenau and Preuß were in senior government positions, and they were Jewish."

"Do you mean since Herr Hitler gained more power?"

"Well, things have been changing since the Great Depression hit in 1929 and now, yes, things have got worse with Herr Hitler. He has taken the title of *Führer* since Hindenburg died earlier this year. He is picking a fight and he has the power. He is using us and blaming us for all Germany's difficulties, past and present."

"I saw shops with a yellow star." Izzy looked up at Garrit and caught his frown.

"Yes, that was decreed last year. The bigger stores have been ordered to close. Many have been Aryanised." He looked over his shoulder and then leaned into Izzy, whispering in her ear, "Stolen." Then he straightened up. "Many smaller shops may continue, but they must identify themselves if they are Jewish."

"Oh, Garrit. This is all so different, so horrible. Are you safe?"

"Yes, yes. It's not dangerous at all. Not for such as me. I go to work. I come home and help my father and *Mutti*. Ester has her wheelchair, but she needs carrying from one room to another for certain things. She is too heavy for *Mutti*, and my father is working such long hours now. Even more than before." He laughed mirthlessly. "But we are safe. I am not an agitator, I'm afraid. Perhaps I should be, but I have an even quieter life these days and much of my work is done at home anyway."

He placed his hand on the small of her back. Its warmth permeated the soft, fine fabric of her dress, and a small breath escaped her lips. She automatically leaned towards him and looked up. He guided her back towards the little foyer of his building, and once through the door he turned her to face him. Slowly, he reached up and unpinned her hat. Staring at the pin thoughtfully, he pushed it through the fabric before tossing it onto the stairs. All the while, she watched him. His smile was the gentlest, sexiest smile she had ever received.

He leaned down and softly took her face between his hands, before placing his lips against hers. She couldn't help but respond, leaning into him. One arm came around her shoulders while the other caressed her cheek. He pulled her closer and she felt the tip of his tongue pushing, ever so gently, so that she opened her lips to receive it, where it played with her own. He gave a subtle groan and both his arms enfolded her firmly. She'd never know what would have happened next, because higher up a door banged, and footsteps sounded on the stairs above them. It was her turn to sigh.

In that moment, she knew she loved him above all others, and it would always be so.

Returning to the apartment and his family, Izzy took a seat once more.

"You must be careful coming here, my dear," Garrit's mother said and looked sideways at her son. "Recently there has been a great wave of legislation restricting our people. Since the Law for the Restoration of Professional Civil Service last year, many of us are excluded from state service. There are restrictions for Jewish students in schools, and my husband lost his job as a doctor. I have to say this … you are not one of us. Please understand, we are very happy to see you, but our customs are not yours. Please don't think badly of me for saying these things."

"*Mutti…*" Garrit said, but she held up her hand.

"We love to see you and you are always welcome to visit our home. I say these things because I understand that you and … and my son are good friends, but as I said before, our ways are different to yours."

"I understand, Frau Shain. I am visiting Germany for a short time only. I must care for my elderly father back in England."

Frau Shain smiled at her. "We all have responsibilities, do we not Garrit?"

"I must leave. I am expected back with my friends, who are kindly letting me stay with them. Thank you for your hospitality and your words of wisdom," Izzy said, although she was fuming inside.

At the bottom of the stairs, Garrit took her in his arms and said, "Please forgive my mother. She is old-fashioned and she worries. Times are difficult for us at the moment, but all things pass and I'm sure these will, too. Our people have been persecuted all around the world and throughout history. We will survive."

"Perhaps I should not come again," Izzy ventured, looking up into Garrit's eyes.

"I sincerely hope you will, my dearest Izzy."

"If you want to see me, I shall. Or perhaps we might meet somewhere else?" They made their arrangements before Garrit kissed her. His lips were warm and soft at first, becoming firm and passionate. She leaned against him, aware of his need for her and sure of her own for him.

CHAPTER 17

Yorkshire, 1975

As usual, Heather was in the library with Izzy. She looked across at her, waiting for her to say more. Eventually, she could stand it no longer. "So, you knew you loved him," she prompted. "What happened? I know from school and basic history that things turned very sour."

"Yes." Izzy didn't continue. Sadness clouded her face.

Heather decided not to push her, but silently wondered what had followed. Had Otto done his worst, and had Garrit faced the death camps? Hadn't Izzy told her that Garrit had come to England, though? Why had they not married? Had he returned to Berlin or stayed here?

Heather lay awake that night, turning one way and then the other. Counting butterflies instead of sheep sometimes worked, but not this time. Eventually, she gave up. Throwing back the blankets and putting on her dressing gown, she crept downstairs, avoiding the fourth step from the bottom, which tended to creak. She didn't need her mum just now. She needed space to think.

Had she made a mistake, letting Brian go? Izzy's words came back: "You can't live your life in safe mode without love." Brian could be kind, but he was undeniably the safe option. But when she had gone for the exciting option, Kev, he had let her down badly. Everyone in the office had known about his affair with Tracey. Everyone except her, and when she'd found out her humiliation had been complete. If she was certain of one thing, it was that Brian would never treat her that way. Oh Lord. Should she phone him tomorrow and grovel? Tell him that she had got herself in a panic and didn't want to break up? Perhaps that would be the best thing. If she missed the highs, at least she'd escape the lows. Life might not be so bad with him.

In the kitchen, Heather put a pan of milk on the gas ring then plonked down on a chair and flicked through a magazine her mum had left on the table. Before long, she smelled the burning milk and heard the hiss as it hit the flame.

Damn! She'd have to clean the mess and start again.

At last, she returned to the table and hunched over the mug of hot cocoa. She'd put in an extra spoon of sugar as a consolation.

I doubt I'll get answers to all my questions tomorrow, Heather thought as she dragged herself upstairs. *I'm in the craft room all morning, and I'm sure Izzy said she was having her hair washed and cut.*

Heather jerked awake when the alarm went off and she groaned. She was on an early shift at The Beeches. Stretching over, she managed to tweak the curtain back and saw a small patch of pale blue. Not quite enough to sew a pair of sailor's trousers, as her granny used to say before she moved to Spain.

Her next thought was Brian. When might be best to phone him? He'd be on his way to work by now. He liked to get there early and crack on before all the others arrived. No good during the morning. She'd need his undivided attention. Lunchtime? Maybe.

Heather reached the care home in good time and entered the craft room. There was only one other person there, and she sat knitting in a wingback chair.

"Morning, dear," she said and smiled.

"Good morning," said Heather. "I'm going to prepare the painting table. Is there anything I can get for you before I do that?"

"No, thanks. I'm up with the lark. Couldn't sleep. It comes with being old."

Heather bent down to open the cupboard. She found it was easier to kneel, get all the things out, and put them up on the work surface above her head. Then she could arrange them. She heard the door open a couple of times and called, "I'm down here. Shan't be a mo. Just getting the art stuff out."

There was quite a bit. Plastic palettes; brushes of different sizes, shape and hair type; watercolour paint; some tubes of acrylic. Then she reached to the back of the cupboard for the wide-based plastic tubs for water. "Oof!" she puffed as she clambered to her feet and brushed a stray hair from her face.

She was greeted by a pair of piercing green eyes and a mischievous grin as Will leant both hands on the other side of the table, leaning forwards. Her heart thudded. She must look a sight, after grovelling on her hands and knees in the cupboard.

"Oh, it's you. Hello," she said.

"Need a hand? I'm not on 'til lunchtime. I came in early to do some painting of my own." Will flashed her a smile.

"I've got it, thanks," Heather said.

As the morning wore on, she chatted with residents, changed water pots for them, and made a round of teas and coffees. She also found herself watching Will out of the corner of her eye.

He fascinated her. Sometimes he was frowning as he concentrated. Once or twice he stood back with his head to one side, regarding his work. Sometimes she could only see the top of his head over the easel. All the time, she wondered about the girl in the painting — who she was and what she meant to him.

Several times he caught her looking and grinned. Heather disapproved. He shouldn't be flirting with her if he already had romance in his life. The girl had to be a lover, surely. He was painting her with such care and attention to detail.

"Do you want to see this?" he asked.

Heather's head shot round. Heat spread up her neck, and she was cross with herself for reacting so.

"It's just that you keep looking," Will added.

"Go on," one of the residents said and gave her a little shove.

She had no choice. "I might as well," she said and shrugged. Then she thought that she sounded ungracious, so she gave a tight little smile and tried to look apologetic.

The painting had progressed quite a long way since her illicit peek before. The leaves and berries in the background gave the piece an autumnal look, which complemented the auburn-haired girl.

Heather was speechless for several moments, and she was hyperaware of Will standing next to her. He smelled of linseed and lemon and he towered above her, her head being level with his shoulder.

"Well?"

She turned and looked up at him. For once, he didn't seem so confident. His expression was anxious.

"It's incredible." Heather was amazed. "She has a look of *Fiammetta*."

"*Fiammetta*! Boccaccio's *Little Flame*. But little flames don't last long enough," he said quietly.

Heather was puzzled. She'd never heard of Boccaccio, and only knew of Dante Gabriel Rossetti's painting because they'd been introduced to it at school.

Then Will's mood changed, and he chuckled. "I wish I was as good as Rossetti. Still, I enjoy it, and this little lady will be pleased, I think."

"I'm sure she will." Heather nodded. "She looks stunning."

"She can be. She can also be a little demon, but I love her all the same."

Heather was surprised to feel a stab of envy. "Ah, there's the ten-minute warning dinner gong," she said hurriedly. "I must clear up. I'm helping in the dining room today."

Despite some prevarication on her part, Heather and Will left the room together and walked side by side down the corridor to the lift. She folded her arms and stayed silent, unsure what to say and not wanting to encourage him in any way. When she took a quick peek at him, he grinned at her. His proximity was still disturbing, but not in the same way as before. Since her discovery of his interest in the badgers and his uncertainty regarding his artistic talent, Heather no longer saw Will as arrogant. She didn't trust him, though. There was still the issue of him snooping in the office and this beautiful girlfriend of his. She sighed.

All too soon, the lift stopped and the doors opened. They were both busy for the next hour, and lunchtime came and went in a flash.

Heather was busy all afternoon too, and it wasn't until she went to retrieve her bicycle that she realised she hadn't rung Brian. Somehow, she no longer wanted to.

Will came around the corner of the building as she was putting the elastic bands around her wide trouser legs to prevent them catching in her bike chain. Her helmet still swung from the handlebars. *Thank goodness I haven't put it on yet*, she thought. *It's so unattractive.* She quickly chided herself. *What does that matter? Really!*

"I wondered if you're busy tonight," Will said, fiddling with the bucket handle he carried.

"What?" Heather spluttered, then she realised how rude that sounded. "Sorry. Pardon?"

"Do you fancy going for a drink?"

She suddenly felt lightheaded and weak-kneed, and there was several moments of silence between them.

"Look, if you'd rather not... Maybe there's already someone special in your life. Perhaps we got off on the wrong foot, although I'm truly unsure how or why. Forget I asked."

CHAPTER 18

Heather stood a couple of doors down from the White Horse, twisting the middle button on her jacket. Then she moved her bag from one shoulder to the other and looked up and down the street.

Was this all another terrible mistake? She deliberately hadn't arrived early, and now she was here alone. Had she been stood up? That would be the ultimate insult. She blew out her cheeks. This was a right slap in the face. One more look at her watch, and then she'd be off. There was a whiff of vinegar and fish from the shop up the road. Her tummy rumbled. She'd been busy getting ready and had only slurped half a mug of tea.

Will was turning out to be just what she'd thought. A jerk. Why hadn't she listened to her head? He was not to be trusted on any front. That business in the matron's office had never really been sorted out. What the hell was she doing here? How could she have been so stupid?

As she was digging around in her bag for a polo mint, she concluded that this was a waste of time. She would go home and lick her wounds yet again.

A voice broke into her anger. He was here, at last. "I'm so sorry. I got held up at home. You must think me so rude."

"Yes, I was about to go." Heather didn't care that she sounded grouchy.

"You have every right to be cross. But I am really sorry; it was something I honestly couldn't leave."

She shrugged, only slightly mollified.

"A drink, and I'll even buy you crisps to make up for it." He laughed, but she scowled at him. She wasn't going to let him off that easily. "Actually, have you eaten since lunchtime?"

"No. I didn't have time; I was having a bath and getting ready."

"There's that new place in Lion Square. The Italian. They do pizza. It's very good. I'll take you there. To say sorry."

"I've heard of pizza and seen it in American films, but I've never had one."

"I'm sure there will be spaces midweek. Let's go, then. I'm starving." Will grabbed her hand.

"Hang on. I haven't said I will, yet. I'm not sure."

"Okay. I've said I'm sorry, and I am. I'm happy to buy you supper as a penance. Then we can leave it at that. You can't lose, and I'll never pester you again." He shrugged.

"Mmm." Heather heaved a sigh. "All right. Thank you."

He hurried her along. She almost had to trot to keep up. Perhaps he was worried she'd change her mind. Well, this was all it was going to be. He could pay for her supper and then … goodbye.

The warmth of his long fingers around hers seemed natural, so she didn't snatch her hand away but extricated herself after a few steps.

As they walked, Heather wondered how he knew about pizzas and Italian restaurants. Is this where he brought his girlfriend?

"We came here for my sister's birthday a month ago," Will said, as if reading her mind.

"I see," was all she said.

"I am really sorry. I had to help my mum and sister with something."

She supposed family values were a positive.

It wasn't long before they were seated. The room was intimately lit with wall lights, and great frescos adorned the spaces between them, illustrating what Heather imagined were scenes from Italy. Roman-looking buildings and scenes of olive trees and rolling hills were painted with delicate brushstrokes. The tables were covered with crisp white cloths and a dark-haired waiter placed a serviette across Heather's lap with a flourish.

"To drink, *signorina*? I can recommend a light white wine I think you will enjoy." He flashed her a smile before he turned to Will. "Unless, sir, you have a preference."

"Perhaps we might see the wine list and menu." Will took control with ease.

"Of course, *signore*." The waiter bowed his head.

Will looked at Heather and winked. She burst out laughing. The ice having been broken, they began to chat. She found herself telling him about her father.

"He called me Heather Honey, but he still left when I was only thirteen. Mind you, he was very strict and if I went out, even to the church youth club, I had to be in by nine at the very latest. He came looking for me once. I was nearly home, but I was with a group of friends. It was so embarrassing. I wasn't allowed to go again for a month. All because I was ten minutes late. It's just Mum and me now."

"I live with Mum and my sister. My dad died when I was fifteen, so things are similar in a way."

"The man of the house, then."

"I suppose so, yes."

"How old is your sister? What's her name?"

"Stella. She's seventeen, but she's younger in many ways."

"Not streetwise? That's a good thing, I should think."

"No, not that."

"Is she still at school?"

"No, she left when she was sixteen. She goes to a training place."

"What's she training to be?"

"This and that; cooking and stuff." He shrugged and she didn't pursue it.

Music that sounded like a mandolin softly played in the background, and the wine eased Heather's mood. They talked of music they each liked. She'd been to see Wings in Manchester a couple of years ago. He was envious. He'd been to Earl's Court in London that same year, to see Pink Floyd and had played their LP of *The Dark Side of the Moon* almost non-stop since then.

"No, you didn't? Wow!" Heather exclaimed.

They chattered about holidays, or lack of them. Neither had been very far. They asked each other's ages, eventually, and discovered there were two years between them. He'd had to repeat a year at school and retake his exams because of his father's death. He'd worked at The Beeches for three years after going to art school for three years. He was vague about why he did this job when he had been to college and gained qualifications.

Heather didn't tell him about Kev, but she did say a little about Brian. She shared Izzy's wise words with him, and he agreed.

They haggled over the bill, but Will won, repeating it was his apology, and Heather had to give in gracefully.

When they left the restaurant, the light had faded but it was only halfway through the evening. Heather was twisting the button on her jacket again. "Thank you. That was a lovely … pizza."

"Can we do this, well, something similar, soon?" Will took her hand and stilled its motion.

"Will." She hesitated. "It's … I have enjoyed this evening, but maybe we shouldn't repeat it. After all, there's the girl in the painting. You said you loved her, and I know what it's like to be cheated on. I shouldn't have come tonight, but I thought we were just going for a drink. Colleagues and all that. I'm newish to The Beeches. You were being friendly and trying to repair a bad start but…"

He laughed. "I'm not seeing anyone else." He must have caught her quizzical look. "It's true. Come with me. It's not far, I promise. I want, no I *need*, to show you something. Please?" His pleading eyes softened Heather's resolve.

She was totally unsure now and sighed.

"Don't frown," he said. "You'll be perfectly safe."

He took a couple of steps. Heather followed, since he still held her hand, albeit very gently. "Where are we going?"

"Meadow Close. It's really not far."

"I'm not coming in to see your etchings, if that's what you're thinking." Heather tried to make light of her words by smiling up at him.

Will threw his head back and gave a full-throated laugh. "Very good, but no, you're not. Something far better."

They walked on in silence for several minutes, past the fish and chip shop, the gift shop, two estate agents and a small charity shop before they rounded the corner and took the second turn on the right into a small close with bungalows in a row. Each had a tiny garden in the front. They stopped outside the gate to number 7.

"This is where I live with my mum and my sister. I'd like you to come in and say hello."

Heather looked at him in the yellow light of the streetlamp and saw his pleading expression. Intrigued, she could do nothing else but precede him through the gate and up the short path. A soft glow came from the window of the room next to the front door. He had his key out ready and he let them into a long hallway with doors on each side.

"Is that you, our Billy?" A voice came from beyond one of them.

"No, Mum, it's a burglar," he shouted back. "I'm here to pillage." He looked at Heather, raised his eyes and shook his head.

She giggled. "Billy?"

"Okay, okay, but I'm Will to everyone else."

He took Heather's jacket and hung it on an old-fashioned wooden hallstand. It sat back in an alcove so that the hall itself was quite wide. The carpet was worn in places but looked clean, and the walls had anaglypta paper painted cream. Heather couldn't help noticing that all along one side there was a scuff mark, about two feet from the floor. He saw she'd noticed but made no reference to it.

Heather took a quick look in the mirror and tried to tame her hair after the walk from the restaurant. It was always a wild, curly riot. People thought she'd had a perm in the latest fashion, but she had no need.

"It's fine," Will said, watching her. "Lovely, in fact. Come in, I want you to meet my mum, Debra, and my sister will be in here, too." He opened the first door on the left. "Mum, this is Heather from work." Will went in first and Heather stood in the doorway.

There was no carpet on the floor in this room, but the boards were shiny, the furniture sparse and well-spaced.

"Lovely to meet you at last." Debra stood as Heather entered. "I've been hearing so much about you."

Heather's reaction, of course, was one of puzzlement.

"Come on in. Don't stand on ceremony."

Will guided Heather forwards. He then turned and indicated the far end of the long room where a small dining table was placed, upon which was a tray with a puzzle. A girl sat before it in a wheelchair, which she manoeuvred round and brought towards them.

Heather was stunned into silence. The vivid auburn hair of the girl hung around her narrow shoulders, and her eyes were large and stunning. Their extraordinary colour was emphasised by her pale skin. Heather knew this face. Will had captured it perfectly in his painting.

"This is my sister, Stella." Will flourished his hand.

"*Fiammetta*," Heather whispered.

CHAPTER 19

England, 1938

Mr Strong was getting on in years, and when Izzy wasn't busy running the house to ensure her father's comfort and wellbeing, she was at one of her women's groups. She was one of several to teach rug-making to the unemployed; she helped with encouraging a rural community at a local village to preserve food in case of war, which seemed increasingly likely; she supported at a day nursery for the children of factory workers. She hardly had a spare minute, but she also managed to assist her sister Rose with some basic administrative work at the school. Often this was done during the evenings at home. After all, she had nowhere else to go and no one else to be with. Her life was full of activity, but none of it for herself. She was no martyr, but she had resigned herself to being the spinster daughter who was needed at home.

She was now nearer to forty than thirty. Delphi was still in France with Rainier, and Rose was happy with Michael and her huge family of other peoples' children. Every day Izzy thought about Garrit. Had she missed an opportunity? Possibly. Probably.

She worried about the situation developing in Germany. Garrit had said they would be safe there, in Berlin. In January of the previous year, Jewish people's property had been seized, and owners had been forced without legal basis to sell their businesses, in most cases at well below the accepted value. Garrit apparently kept a quiet life and went out rarely, but on 30th May last year there had been a *Razzia* against Jews that had taken place in the streets for all to see. There were stories of the SS assuming control of a home for children who were disabled and that a programme of euthanasia had been adopted. An article Izzy read said that a concentration camp had been opened at a place called Buchenwald near Weimar. Half the Jewish population had fled the country, many going to Palestine. Izzy knew Garrit had no desire to go there. He was Jewish, but not a strict practitioner. And now there were even restrictions in place for that destination.

"Rose, I'm so worried about the Shain family in Germany," Izzy said to her sister.

"Michael was talking about it only last night. We listened to a recital on the radio. Laella Finnsburg was the soprano. Very good."

Izzy was irritated. *Who cares about a music programme?*

Rose continued, "Then he turned over and we caught the news. These raids in the streets of Berlin sound very bad."

"I've been racking my brain about what I might do to help them. With all these people coming here, to England, surely there must be a way to help the Shain family."

"Yes, but there's talk of tightening the regulations because of the numbers coming."

"Garrit wrote some time ago and told me he has money in a bank here."

"Really? That was very forward-thinking of him."

"I imagine he could see what was happening all around him. There has been a whole raft of new laws and regulations, all designed to punish and limit how the Jewish population survive."

"Money here might help. One of the new rules is that immigrants must have fifty pounds deposited here. But now Germany's not letting people take money out of the country."

"That's a huge amount. I don't know if he has that much. It's a bit money-grabbing of our government when people are in such dire circumstances. These people are in danger. There are four of the Shain family, too."

"No country can take half another's population, darling. It's not possible."

"I know." Izzy sighed and wanted to weep.

"Garrit's sister has cerebral palsy, didn't you say?"

"She's wheelchair-bound, but her brain's sharp."

"And what of the parents? What sort of age are they?"

"Age? I'm not sure. Not young, of course, but younger than Papa, I think. He's a doctor. I'm sure he would qualify if he had the money. I know it's against the law over there to have foreign currency now, but maybe with his profession our government might waive the rules. She's a housewife and very hardworking. Have you a plan?"

"Perhaps we could act as guarantors and sponsor them. They could work here in the school for their bed and board. They would only be allowed over here for a limited time. Some people come as transit visitors while they await visas and permissions to go onto somewhere else like America."

"Oh, that wouldn't suit."

"I know, I know. You want them here. I understand. That's what we'll go for first. I'm sure the rules state they're expected to return to Germany as soon as they can, though. The sister might be difficult, Izzy."

"She could do many jobs, I'm sure."

"I'm sympathetic to that, darling." Rose put her hand on Izzy's arm. "You must know I am, but there are laws and rules."

"Time is running out. I'm worried, Rose."

"I'll speak to Michael. He's taking Latin class now, with the older ones, but as soon as he's finished, I'll catch him."

"Thank you."

After luncheon, Rose sought Izzy again, and by then Izzy was in a very fretful state. She had hunted through the old newspapers in the boot room but only found minimal snippets of information about the current situation.

"Michael spoke with the Duke of Norfolk on the telephone. He's been very helpful."

"The number of times I've cursed him for letting this place to you, especially when you were so ill… I take it all back now, if he's prepared to help. Tell me, what has Michael found?"

"He said it was very difficult because the government are reluctant to issue information."

"But why?"

"Cynically, the Home Secretary can be as restrictive or compassionate as he chooses, I suppose, but things are changing. Now the Home Office are going to be insisting on visas for all new immigrants very soon. Since the Aliens Act after the last show, there have been restrictions on who can come. There's only so many poor people we can accommodate. Now, there has been such a wave of people escaping this tyranny…"

"I know, but what does this mean for Garrit and his family? They have much to offer."

"It means we need to move fast, my dear."

"Will Michael sponsor them, then?" Izzy forced herself to be calm and took a deep breath, sitting upright in her chair.

"Domestic help is one of the categories listed on the shortage occupations list, so we would be prepared to act as guarantors for that. It seems little to offer, but at least they would be safe. They might need to have some kind of assimilation, we understand."

Izzy was puzzled.

"They would have to agree to not speak German here, for example, and to follow our ways. Honestly, Izzy, these are the regulations, not our rules. You know we will be sympathetic. You'll need to get in touch with Garrit as soon as possible and tell him to arrange travel. I fear time is running out before laws here are changed and before the situation over there becomes more difficult. We will start things moving from this end."

"There are Quakers in Vienna and in Berlin who might help them, I've heard."

"They need to hurry."

Now that Izzy had thought about all this in detail and it seemed as if there might, just might, be a resolution, she was beside herself with terror that something would happen to prevent Garrit and his family from coming to England. She had loved him for so long, but she had been unable to leave her responsibilities and he had needed to stay in Germany for his mother and sister. Their lives were a mirror and neither had been brave enough, or selfish enough, to follow their dreams. If they all came to England, though, how different things might be.

Izzy tried to throw all her energies into her activities. She couldn't concentrate, making silly mistakes in her typing, allowing the milk to boil over onto the range, missing parts of conversations. Each day was interminable as she waited for a response to her letter to Garrit. Her imagination began to conjure problems and scenarios of impending doom. Trains were impossible to book, soldiers came before they could leave, Ester caught a fever and could not travel.

Eventually, Izzy received a card telling her that Garrit had met someone from the Quaker community. It did not detail what arrangements, if any, he had been able to make. It did say that his mother and father were very 'occupied with business' and could not take a holiday. She didn't know what that meant. It sounded like some coded message, and she guessed they would not be coming. This sent her into a further frenzy. What if Garrit was 'occupied' too?

CHAPTER 20

England, 1939

The last six months had disappeared in a blink. Garrit and Ester had made it to England. Ester was working at the school in the laundry room, and was liked by the staff because of her sunny, self-effacing, friendly manner. She did her best to speak English, albeit in a basic way and had made good progress. Garrit did odd jobs, mending things, cleaning. Izzy thought it was demeaning when he had such a good brain. She had spoken to Michael about allowing him to teach the languages in which he was so proficient, but it would put someone else out of work, and teaching German was not to be contemplated in the current circumstances.

Izzy knew the pair would be thinking of their parents, who had indeed opted to remain in Germany, convinced they would be safe although living in dire conditions. Herr Shain was a doctor, after all, and they kept a very low profile so he could continue to help those in desperate circumstances.

One Sunday morning, they were all gathered around the wireless. The voice of BBC Radio, Alvar Lidell, had just announced that the Prime Minister would speak to the nation. Rose took Michael's hand and Garrit took Ester's. Oh, how Izzy wanted him to clutch hers like that. She was all alone in this small company.

Then Neville Chamberlain's live broadcast started, and silence blanketed the little group. "This morning, the British ambassador in Berlin handed the German government a final note..." Izzy shivered and realised she had missed some of the message. "I have to tell you now that no such undertaking has been received, and that consequently this country is at war with Germany…"

Within moments of the speech ending, they heard an air-raid siren in the distance and a single bell tolled in the village. They looked at each other in silence before Michael and Rose got up.

"I must go to see the children," Michael said.

"Yes, we must ensure they're not distressed and that the staff are coping," Rose added.

Izzy had such a heavy lump in her chest that she found it difficult to breathe. "I must return to Papa. It was very thoughtful of him to insist I come here." She glanced at Garrit. "He only has old Dora. He sent Betty home."

"Wait, please, one moment." Garrit watched as Rose and Michael left the room. Izzy saw him squeeze Ester's hand as he said to her, "I'll catch you up."

When they were alone, he came towards Izzy. She took him in her arms, guessing how fearful he must be. His breath left him in a gust, and he shuddered.

"Now I truly dread the worst, having heard and seen so much terror already," he whispered into her hair. "*Mutti* and Papa will be lucky to come out of this." He paused to gather himself, but his next words came out almost as a sob. "I fear we will not see them again."

The first time Izzy came to Garrit, she believed she was destined to be his and cared not about the future. There may not be one. As she knocked softly on his door, her ear was almost pressed to the white-painted wood. Her breathing was shallow as she waited for a response. She nearly changed her mind. Then the handle turned and the door opened a little.

Garrit smiled when he saw her.

Izzy needed his arms around her. She wanted so much more. He had told her he loved her many times. Her fingers tingled with her need to hold his face, be aware of the prickle of his skin in her palms. She loved the dark shadows of his face at this time of day and his black hair, now with a few strands of grey beginning to show at his temples. She felt an urge to run her fingers through its denseness. When his deep brown eyes looked at her, her insides plunged, making her forget what she was doing.

Garrit said nothing when he saw her, but opened the door wider. After a quick glance over her shoulder, she slipped into his room. Then, unsure of herself, she stood before him and looked up. He must have sensed the longing on her face because he leaned down and kissed her slowly, carefully. "Are you sure?" he whispered, and she nodded.

His hand reached down and slid up under her skirt to the top of her stockinged thigh. Her body arched towards him and he groaned softly.

Then she took fright and pulled back.

"I'm sorry, so sorry," he said. "I thought…"

Paralysed by indecision, she looked up and saw tears glistening in his eyes. Then she knew. She wanted to kiss his neck and lean against his body with the full length of her own. She wanted to be enveloped by it, by him; she wanted to wrap her legs around him so he could never leave her.

In his room, they were protected from the outside world. Everyone else was busy with the day. He had finished his morning tasks, and there were two whole hours before he was required to go and start his cleaning jobs and she must return to Papa and supervise his midday meal.

Garrit had discarded his jacket and his shirt sleeves were rolled up, exposing the tanned skin of his forearms, which were covered in a smattering of dark hair that crept down to the backs of his hands. Izzy's fingers trembled as she undid the top few buttons of his shirt, exposing his chest. He wore no vest, and her breath caught in her throat. He took one of her hands and kissed her fingers before he kissed her lips again. Then he slowly undid the buttons of her blouse. Reaching around, he unfastened her underwear and cupped one of her small breasts before bending his head to kiss her there.

CHAPTER 21

Yorkshire, 1975

Heather remained silent, aware that Izzy was lost in her memories. She readjusted her position on the footstool and Izzy was recalled to the present.

"We became lovers," she said in an undertone. "Are you shocked?"

"Goodness me, no. Times may have been different in some ways back then, but..." Heather's words petered out as she became unsure what to say.

"We were uncertain of everything. Living for the moment became a way of life. In 1940 and '41 Manchester took several hits with bombing. Fourteen nurses were killed one night when the old Salford hospital was hit, and a stand at Old Trafford took a direct one and it was destroyed. I used to go there occasionally with Papa when I was a girl. He was quite a big football fan. They were aiming for the industry at Trafford Park, I think. The football team had to play at City's Maine Road stadium. Surprising what allegiances are made in dire times." A gentle smile played at the corners of Izzy's mouth, stretching out the wrinkles that had settled there over the years. "At home we used to hear the waves of bombers passing over. Unmistakeable, and I'll never forget it. A deep rumbling but with a rhythm. So terrifying. I worked in Salford during the war, so I didn't see Garrit too often."

"What did you do in Salford?"

"I worked in a day nursery for factory workers. It was long hours, seven in the morning until seven at night, and I often slept over with the other girls. Goodness, it was tough. Not as bad as the factory itself, of course. Those girls had an awful job, but the little ones... Each morning, we had to de-louse them."

"Oh!"

"Yes, well, the mothers came from the poorest places. I had no training. I didn't even have my school certificate because I'd been back and forth to Germany, even before the first long stay I'd had with Gisela. Papa had allowed Rose to go to Oxford and Delphi had joined the WAACs during the first show, but when it was my turn, I wanted to go to Germany to finish my education. Anyway, in 1940 the government were crying out for women to help, so the Ministry of Labour encouraged women into work. That's what I did. I was an assistant at a day nursery. It meant I could still help Rose and keep an eye on the domestic staff who looked after Papa." Izzy laughed. "If I ever smell cod liver oil, it takes me straight back to that time. Even after a boil wash, the children's little overalls had the odour from where they'd dribbled it back out.

"When I did meet Garrit alone, it was often in the woods around the field from the school. There was a grassy glade and it was surrounded by bushes. Out of bounds to pupils, so quite safe for us. I'm too old to take my shoes off and walk across the grass here now, but I often think I'd like to. Back then, it was cool between my toes and oddly liberating. If it was too cold, sometimes we would meet in his room, but not often. It wasn't easy."

"Would you have been in disgrace back then?"

"Probably. Oh, yes. We were both frightened to marry, you see. We discussed it endlessly. Garrit always said it was a grand adventure to be a refugee, at first, anyway. Nothing bad happened to him, as it did to those at home. He spoke often of his parents and not knowing where they were. He would have to go back after the war. Sponsorship for him to escape the Nazis was on that condition, and he had his parents to find. The news from there became worse and worse. I had Papa to look after. I couldn't have gone with Garrit, or so I thought. We squandered our opportunity. A sad and almost wicked thing to have done. We constructed walls of false reasoning around ourselves." Izzy sat in a reverie once more, and then her eyelids drooped and she slept.

As Heather lay in bed that night, she tossed and yawned. Izzy's words turned around in her head. *We squandered our opportunity ... a sad and almost wicked thing to have done... Squandered...* She shouldn't squander her life by constructing walls around herself and playing it safe. She had to reach out and grasp opportunities. But was Will an opportunity, or another disaster waiting to claim her? He had good family values, but could he be trusted? The old insecurity returned. She was frightened of making another mistake.

Time to take control. She huffed and turned once more, then threw back the covers. Pulling open the curtains, she gazed into the night. All colour was drained away. There were some clouds, and a thin crescent moon cast shadows in the tiny garden where flowers bobbed in the breeze. Puddles in the road from an earlier shower ruffled, distorting reflections from orange streetlamps. She was all alone and it was depressing.

She found her dressing gown and decided a mug of hot cocoa might help — her go-to when troubled.

As she sat hunched at the table with her hands around her mug, she went through the events of the previous evening. Finding out that the much-loved girl from the painting was Will's sister, and that she was wheelchair-bound, was a surprise to say the least. That he was close to her and helped with her care was also a revelation. Loyalty and responsibility were admirable characteristics. But what of his sneaking in Mrs Friend's office? She still couldn't quite dismiss that. She hadn't been aware of further incidents, but then how would she know? He could have been in there any number of times on the pretext of cleaning. Perhaps he was taking small amounts of money. Maybe he was spying on his employer.

She sat up straighter as the door opened and her bleary-eyed mum entered.

"Couldn't sleep, love?"

"No. Things whirring around in my brain. Daft, really." Heather tried to sound light-hearted.

"Anything in particular? Sometimes it helps to share. Remember when you used to have that recurring nightmare when you were little? As soon as we found out and you told us the details, it stopped. So, what's the problem tonight?"

"It's this bloke Will from the care home. I enjoyed the time out with him, and he surprised me in some ways." Heather explained about the evening and his sister but added that she was concerned about his trustworthiness.

"Only one way to find out. Ask him outright what he was doing there, picking through stuff. Watch his face as he answers. Nowt ever wrong with talking. Mostly, we don't do it enough. It can solve many a problem. That *is* something I've learned over the years. I've often wondered whether your dad may have eased off, if I'd told him outright how overbearing he was. I gave him permission, with my silence, to carry on and get worse."

"Do you miss him?"

"Not these days. At first, I missed having another adult around, but since you've grown up, what more could I want?

Having you living here again is wonderful, but I know at some point you'll find another place of your own. That's as it should be, and it'll be fine. In the meantime, talk to Will!" She fetched herself a glass of water and kissed Heather on the top of her head. "Right, I'm off to bed. Sleep tight, my love."

"Thanks, Mum." Heather watched June disappearing through the door. They were increasingly close now she was older herself. How lucky she was. Talking and sharing was indeed a good thing, she decided.

She rinsed her mug, tucked her chair under the table and went back to bed. She descended into a deep sleep, until the alarm woke her with a start.

As she propped her bike against the wall of the care home, Heather glanced at the bushes from which Will had emerged that night. The thick glossy leaves shone in the early morning sunlight but there was no rustling or cracking of twigs now, and no Will emerging with a frown. She still couldn't make him out. Conceited or caring? Deceitful or reliable? Which was the real Will or was he all of these things? She must find out and talking to him might be the best thing to do. Heather spent the morning cleaning out cupboards in the residents' kitchenette, because the girl who was employed to do that had announced her pregnancy and left without warning.

"Since the reorganisation last year, we take five NHS-funded residents, so social services have a right to come in and inspect from time to time," Mrs Friend, the matron, had explained to Heather. "It needs doing regardless of that, though. Joanna walking out couldn't have come at a worse time."

"It's all right, I don't mind," Heather said.

So there she was on her hands and knees, wiping out a cupboard of pots and pans. She certainly didn't want Will walking in now and seeing her backside up in the air, or her dishevelled and sweaty state. Damn, she was thinking about him way too much.

By the time she had finished, it was lunchtime and she still hadn't seen Will. She hurried into the dining room and looked around, but there was no sign of him. She had no idea what his working hours were today, but she had expected to see him there and fix a time to talk. Trying to swallow her disappointment, Heather pasted on a smile as she chatted to the residents at her table.

In the afternoon, she was in the library when Izzy came in. Heather brightened but then saw she was accompanied by another lady. After greeting her with nods and smiles, they sat together chatting, and so Heather was frustrated there too. She would have loved to hear more of Izzy's story.

By the time her shift finished, Heather was thoroughly disgruntled, and she pushed her bike down the drive with a heavy heart.

"What are you scowling about?" A voice she recognised came from the rhododendron bushes lining the long driveway. The broad, waxy leaves swayed, and noisy feet on the dried twigs announced the approach of Will. When he emerged, he was pushing a wheelbarrow. All day he'd been on her mind and she had wanted to speak to him. Now he was here, she had no wish to confront him. She wasn't prepared.

"What on earth are you doing in there at this time of day?" Heather asked.

"I raked the lawn, trimmed the edges of the beds and dead-headed, so I was dumping all the dead petals and bits in amongst the bushes. They'll compost down."

"I didn't see you at lunch."

"Er … no. I had it at home. Late shift today. Is that why you're frowning so?" He gave her a wink and a cheeky grin. "Did you miss me that much?"

Heather huffed but was aware of heat creeping up her neck. She bent to adjust her bicycle clip at her ankle and then unhooked her helmet from the handlebars and fiddled with the strap. Anything to avoid eye contact.

"Sorry." Will tried to look serious as she straightened up. "What is it?"

She took a gulp of air. "I wanted to ask you something."

"Ask away." His brow creased into a small frown.

"Um, well, not here and you're busy."

"'Fraid I don't finish until nine this evening."

"Never mind, then. It can wait."

He shrugged. "Right. I'll see you tomorrow, then. And put that on. Much safer." He nodded at the helmet she was turning around in her hands.

"Yes, bye." She did as she was told and as he pushed his barrow up the drive, she got on her cycle and headed home.

CHAPTER 22

A couple of days later Heather stood alone in the little kitchen at The Beeches, making herself a cup of tea. The door opened and she glanced over her shoulder. When she saw who it was, her breath left her lungs in a rush.

"Oh, it's you," she croaked.

"I've come to check a plug socket. It's loose, apparently." Will had a screwdriver in his hand. "You wanted to ask me something the other day." He knelt on the floor, his back to her. This helped — she didn't have to look him in the eye.

"Er … yes." She turned and leaned against the worktop, her hands gripping its edge. "Look, it's about what you were doing in the matron's office after I first arrived here."

"I see. Right." He turned and his green eyes pierced her.

"Well?"

"You want to know what I was up to? I wasn't thieving, you know. That's what you thought, wasn't it?"

She paused. "Yes, if you must know. The cash box was right there, and it was open."

"And I wasn't looking for details of wills so I would know who to target to leave their riches to me, either." Will stood and turned, hands on his hips, but he was smiling.

The sun streaming in through the window highlighted the blond beard beginning to grow on his chin. His hair was shiny and curled on his collar. Heather was almost distracted…

She put on a frown. "So…?" Now she'd started, she was determined to get to the bottom of it. She folded her arms.

His answer was not what she expected. "Okay. I heard from a friend of a friend that there were plans to sell the home and build on the site. It was pub talk, and there may be nothing in it. I thought there might be some paperwork around that would either confirm or deny the rumour. It's such a great local resource for the old folk, never mind the wildlife in the woods at the back."

"But that's dreadful." Heather pulled out a chair from under the small table and plonked down. "Izzy's only just arrived. She's becoming settled. It would be awful. Where would they all go?" She turned to him. "Did you find anything?"

"Not really. There was a letter from a business brokers called Dakins, but it could have been about anything."

"If it's true, then a firm like Dakins might handle it, but not necessarily. It could be a private sale, and then it would all just go through a solicitor. Big corporate companies, and all that. Have you asked anyone?"

"No. I wasn't sure what to do. I need this job, too."

"Let's just ask Mrs Friend. Her reaction may tell us something."

"Yes, you're right, of course. I began to think I was making something out of nothing. It was just something someone said over a pint."

"But it's the residents' wellbeing, lots of people's jobs, even the wildlife, like you said. Come on. Let's go and ask her now." Heather's bravery was beginning to grow as her anger took over. How careless of peoples' lives some companies could be when in search of profit.

By the time they stood outside Mrs Friend's door, they were both breathless. Will knocked.

There was a muffled, "Come in." When they opened the door, Mrs Friend looked at them with surprise. "Hello. Can I help?"

Heather looked at Will.

"I heard a rumour, Mrs Friend," he said. "Someone was saying there's a plan to sell this place and build houses on the site."

Mrs Friend's eyes slid away and she cleared her throat. "Where did you hear this?"

Heather's heart beat a little faster. "Is it true?" she demanded.

"It's all highly confidential," said the matron. "I understand the owner has sought someone out to make a planning application, but it hasn't got that far yet. When, *if*, one is made, the planning office will ask for any comments and it goes from there."

"But this is dreadful. What about all the residents? And all the staff?" Heather raised both her arms in horror.

"This will finish many of them. And the woodland at the back? What about the wildlife?" Will added.

"It's far too early to say. You can imagine this is a shock for me too."

"When will it go to the next stage?"

"Soon, I suppose. The owners will have to pay redundancy to some of the staff. Others won't qualify because of the number of hours they work, or the length of time they've been here." Mrs Friend glanced at Heather miserably.

"It's the residents, mainly. It cannot be allowed to happen," Will said, leaning forward and putting both hands on the edge of the desk.

"Will, I understand, I do. It's a worry for us all, but please…" Mrs Friend trailed off. It seemed too much for her to cope with. "I'm speaking to the owners almost daily about it. As soon as there is more information, I'll let you know."

"I don't think I care to wait for that." Will stood up and folded his arms. "I think I'm going to get to work today, to put a stop to all this before it goes any further."

"I'll certainly support you," Heather said. She was really frightened now.

"I have to be a little careful," Mrs Friend said.

"No, you don't." Will leaned forward again. "You have to decide which side you're on. We cannot let this happen." With that, he turned and left the room.

Heather nodded at Mrs Friend and followed him, closing the door after her. She trotted after Will's retreating figure. "Will, wait."

"Sorry." He stopped and turned. "I'm so angry."

"What will we do?"

"I suppose we'll start with a petition. There are any number of people we can call upon. I have a friend who works for a solicitor. I'll ask him for an opinion." He placed his hand on her arm. "Thanks," he said.

She looked at his long brown fingers and covered them with her own. Tears threatened to overflow. "This affects us all," she said quietly.

As Will looked down, he gently wiped her eyes with his thumb. "We'll win this," he said. "You'll see."

Her cup of tea long-forgotten, Heather hurried along the corridor to Izzy's room. She would not mention this latest development, but she had a yearning to visit the old lady and to know that her friend was comfortable.

She knocked softly on the open door in case Izzy was asleep, but she found her in one of her favourite spots, gazing out of the window. She was hunched in the high-back chair, and her lilac woollen scarf was around her shoulders, despite the warmth of the day. She looked like a little grey rabbit.

As Heather drew near, the old lady turned, and her eyes were lively. "This is such a lovely garden," she said. "I'm so lucky to be here, and very pleased we met. How are you today, my dear?"

"I'm fine, thank you. It is beautiful. Just look at those flowers. I don't know many of their names, but the colours are stunning."

"I like the stirring of rose petals. Like a ruffled collar I had on a day dress once. Just that shade of dark pink. I used to wear a band of the same fabric around my hair, and Garrit said it framed my face like a painting. He was so good at saying just the right thing when I needed to hear it."

"Was that after he came to England?"

"Mmm, I can't remember. It was so long ago. It may have been in Berlin after the war."

CHAPTER 23

England, 1946

Izzy knew that Garrit's position in England was temporary. That was the condition of his sponsorship. Nevertheless, she had always hoped that he and Ester would apply to stay. After all, the war had dragged on, and they had been here for years. He'd had no contact with his parents. This was why Izzy's relationship with him was fraught at times. He was determined to return to his homeland to search for them and she desperately wanted him to stay. Could they not be married? They could return to Germany for a short time and then come home to England, together.

"This is not my home, though, is it?" he said after yet another discussion on the subject. "I have lost my country. I have even lost my language. I am not allowed to speak German here. I am stateless, a non-person. You cannot imagine what that is like. I am demeaned, belittled. To have lost everything is indescribable. My parents have suffered enough. I must find them. I must re-find *myself*, my identity."

"We do not demean you, surely? You are valued. The work you do is important."

"Not you, no, nor your family. I am so grateful to them. It is my situation that takes everything from me."

Izzy hung her head. There was so much strife after such a long and disastrous time. They had all given things up. Could Garrit not see that he could be happy, here with her? She would *make* him satisfied. Fiery anger exploded through her for a second and then dispersed quickly. "You're not a non-person to me," she said quietly. Then she lifted her head and spoke up, although her voice broke as she continued. "You cannot be defined by me alone. You must find your own voice again. I understand, I do."

"Perhaps you do. Dearest Izzy. You know I love you, but I must go home. I must search for my parents. The things we are hearing are a horror story." He paused. "If we marry, you could come to Germany and live as my wife there. You know this. We have spoken of it so many times." His eyes were pleading.

"But I am needed here. Papa has become quite frail and since Rose's TB, things are difficult for her and Michael."

"Others are here to support them. Your Papa will not be here forever. Surely you cannot build your life around him."

Izzy gritted her teeth and held her returning anger at bay. "Exactly. He will not be here forever, but I must make his last years as secure and comfortable as I can. *Surely* you can see that. The situation is so uncertain back in Germany. I mean, the Yalta conference and now Potsdam have not sorted out a viable situation. I don't like the sound of Stalin and now Roosevelt has gone, Truman clearly doesn't trust him either. He still hasn't set up free elections in the east as he promised at Yalta, and that was nearly two years ago. He's even organising a communist government in Bulgaria now the monarchy is abolished, just like in Romania. As for this ten per cent of reparations from the British and American sectors, as well as taking whatever they want from their own zone... It's all broken. How can I possibly come and live over there?" She sighed and placed her hand on his arm. "Perhaps we could visit the British or American zone and stay there while you search for your mother and father, then return here where it is safe."

"I must go to my home, Soviet zone or not. How can I do anything else? I must see for myself what is happening. Yes, Germany and all of Europe is broken, but I can't search for *Mutti und* Papa from a distance."

She refrained from remarking upon the small German slip-up.

"Ester will stay here for a little longer until I can get back to our own home and ensure it is safe for her. Then you could come too. To visit at first, then…" He ran his thumb down her cheek and whispered, "Oh, Izzy. This life is so hard. We each have obligations that we cannot evade. I love you. I always will love you. We will come together when we are able and be grateful for it." He bent his head and softly kissed her lips.

Her arms went around him, and she clung so that his kiss extended. She couldn't release him because if she did, she knew he would be gone, and she didn't know when she would find him again. This moment was all that she had. The strength of his arms, the warmth of his breath upon her cheek, the length of his body against hers.

It was several months before Garrit could return to Germany. There was much document filling and assurances to be made, despite the fact he had his passport from before the war and proof of identity. He contacted the Jewish Relief Unit, who were operating within the British sector. Then he found the United Nations Relief and Rehabilitation Administration was still operating following the Great War but had been subsumed into the United Nations. It took a while to track down relevant departments. They were helping, but some estimates were talking of more than forty million displaced people in Europe alone. People were lost or lacking their roots. It was slightly easier for Garrit, because he had been fortunate enough to have received this sponsorship at the school.

Desperate situations had demanded desperate solutions when the war had ended. Across Europe, displaced people who had performed slave labour had been interred or left wandering. There were stories seeping through of those who did not wish to go to their place of origin being forcibly removed, in some cases brutally, in the eastern regions.

Izzy's worry for Garrit was immense. Even though he was within Western Allied protection, technically he was a displaced person. Newspapers had it that, ironically, thousands of Jews were returning to Germany as a haven. Many hoped to travel on to Palestine, which was fast becoming another huge political crisis, it being thought that some Jews wished to force a partition in that country. Although this was not Garrit's aim, he needed to be sure of his travel plans.

The night before his departure, Izzy fervently prayed that something, anything, would occur to hinder it. She lay in her narrow bed and cried until her eyes stung.

A sliver of light appeared as the door cracked open and Garrit crept to her side. He brushed her hair from her face and stroked her forehead. "Hush, my dearest one, *mein Liebling*."

She sat up and leaned into him, smelling his cologne on the warmth of his body and taking comfort from his arms.

"Shh," he said as he held her. "It won't be long, and you can come to visit me. I am sad to be leaving you for a while, but I must go. You know this. I must find out what has happened to my parents, even though by now I have a good idea. I have tried to be happy, but this eats away at me. I cannot let it go."

"I know it does. I have seen you slipping away from me and becoming like a wraith of who you really are. You need to return to your home. But I'm so desperately sad for all this;

this situation in which we find ourselves. It's so unfair." Izzy's voice broke and a sob escaped.

He stroked her hair again and kissed her forehead. Slowly, she was aware of her body responding to his closeness. A flutter inside stirred and she raised her lips to his. She relaxed a little and moved over as she lay back. He joined her and their kisses became desperate. His lips were hard on hers and her passion for him could not be denied.

Sleep stole all the hurt and worry after anguish lent itself to passionate lovemaking. She awoke as light filled the window and lay still, trying to put off the moment of parting. Garrit lay on his side, one arm lying heavily across her stomach, but she welcomed the weight. She turned her head to look at him. His lips moved as his breath escaped, and Izzy burned the image into her brain. It would have to last for many months.

Perhaps she was being a coward. Was she using her family as an excuse not to face danger and uncertainty abroad? No! She loved this man, but their reliance upon her was real, she persuaded herself. There was no one else to shoulder the responsibility. Delphi had faced dangers of her own in France and now needed to be with her family. Her life was there. Rose was not strong, and Michael was so busy with all that running a successful modern boarding school demanded. Her Papa was increasingly dependent upon her. How could she follow her own desires right now?

Garrit needed to find himself again after his long exile. Izzy couldn't deny him this opportunity. Perhaps they could meet and maybe even become one again, soon. Germany would rebuild with the cooperation of Britain, America and the Soviets. When things became settled there once more, she would join him.

Garrit opened his eyes as she watched him. He gave her a gentle smile. His dark gaze was full of love. She leaned in to kiss him.

"It's morning," she whispered.

"I must go, my love." He kissed her forehead.

He didn't see her tears as he slipped from the bed and crept from her room with only a hasty backwards glance.

CHAPTER 24

The winter of 1946 was brutal, and it lasted well into the new year. The branches of the trees were permanently encased in ice. Grass was crisp and white, and the pavements running up and down the hills were treacherous. Then the snows came to cover them and everything else. In the country districts outside Manchester where Izzy lived with her father, it blew into banks that covered the downstairs windows. Moving about was almost impossible and everyone was cold, undernourished and struggling.

The maid, Betty, and Izzy eventually managed to cut a narrow path through the drifts to the road. After the plough had been through there was a route, of sorts, down into the town, but it was perilous. For those with any sort of ailment or with a pram, it was next to impossible to walk on.

There were huge disruptions to energy supplies because snowdrifts blocked roads and rail links. Many businesses had to close when power was restricted to only a few hours each day. In the north of England animal herds starved or froze to death, and in a country decimated by years of war, this seemed to many like the last straw. Newspapers were reduced in size, magazines had to stop publication and radio broadcasts were limited. Morale quickly declined.

Izzy missed Garrit desperately, but she had to concentrate on surviving. She queued for what seemed like hours for meagre rationed supplies of food, stamping her feet and with her hands in thick mittens. Everyone stood without speaking. Only the odd bout of coughing cracked the silence.

Vegetables froze in the ground and supplies were cut off. Izzy struggled up the hills of her hometown, having managed to buy a paltry, but treasured, couple of pounds of potatoes. As she entered the house, she heard a cough that was familiar. She hurried into the parlour, where her Papa sat huddled under a blanket and Ester did the same. Garrit's sister had been generally unwell for some weeks, looking haggard and grey. She was unable to work at the school and had been transferred to the care of Izzy because Rose couldn't perform nursing duties as well as keeping the school running.

Ester was unable to undertake even the simplest of tasks without collapsing back in her chair, racked with a cough that left her gasping and sweaty. When Izzy looked at her, she dropped her basket and hurried over. Pulling off her mittens, she held her hand to the girl's forehead and then her cheek. Ester was shivering but her temperature was high. Her skin was clammy, and she clutched her chest as the coughing started up again.

"I don't like this," Izzy said. "It sounds bronchial. I'm going to call the doctor."

"Oh no, please don't make a fuss for me. It is expensive, too." Ester was breathless as she spoke. "There will be persons … many worse than me."

"Fuss or no, we've faffed about long enough, lass." She noted Ester's fingernails had a blue tinge, and her thoughts moved from bronchitis to pneumonia. But she was no nurse, and although she had heard stories when she'd worked in the day nursery during the war, she had not had close contact with the illness. "Hush now. If this National Health Service comes into being, it'll be a boon. But right now, hang the expense, I'm calling the doctor."

It was some time before the harassed and overworked doctor managed to arrive. He listened to Ester's chest and took her pulse. She was rushed to the local cottage hospital without further ado, where she had an X-ray. She did indeed have pneumonia, and because of her existing disability it was taken very seriously.

"You're in good company, since Winnie Churchill himself had it not three or four years ago," Izzy said when she visited.

Upon her return to her papa, she said, "They've prescribed sulfathiazole along with potassium citrate, apparently. The one to cure and the other to prevent something or other as a result of the first. It all sounds complicated and serious. Her temperature is reduced, at least. They assure me she will recover, but she'll be weak afterwards for some considerable time."

"That's good news, and a great relief. It's not called 'old man's friend' for nothing, you know."

"What do you mean?"

"You can slip away from this world and into the next before you know it. I saw it many times after the last show when people's resistance was low. There were none of these new antibiotics then. We have a lot for which to thank Mr Fleming, and those who followed him."

"That's cheerful. I thought that was all Spanish flu, after the last war."

"A lot, yes, but not all," Mr Strong said. "Anyway, you say they have caught it in good time?"

"So it seems. She'll need a deal of nursing when she returns." Izzy held in the sigh that threatened to escape. Life was a long, hard struggle. There was no way she would be able to travel any time soon, so going to Germany was out of the question for the time being.

Izzy visited Ester whenever she could, but with no transport because of the state of the roads it added to her daily battles. The pavements on the hills were lethal. Her whole existence was a toil. She just about managed to find enough food for them all. Together with Betty, she cleared snow, she stoked the coal fires, emptied the ashes. She was exhausted.

It was three weeks later when Ester returned to the home of Izzy and her papa. She looked tiny as she sat in her chair, and had little energy for wheeling herself around. Betty had this extra chore to add to her housekeeping duties, but Izzy helped her out in the kitchen, so they managed between them. Papa sat huddled under his blanket, while Izzy wore mittens in the house and had extra layers of clothing. Even so, her chilblains were a further burden, especially at night when her hot water bottle had taken the worst of the raw cold from her bed. The itching on her toes nearly drove her mad as she lay under a great weight of blankets and eiderdown. Ice on the inside of her bedroom window each morning, never mind outside, meant they lived in permanent gloom. The smell from the tiny paraffin heater in the bathroom was awful, but at least it prevented the pipes from freezing overnight.

Ester slowly regained some of her spark and spirit and was determined not to be extra work for anyone, but inevitably she was, and she was far from well enough to travel. Still, it was a huge relief to see her better and her lack of self-pity was a humbling lesson to them all.

Izzy and Garrit had maintained a correspondence of sorts, but letters were often held up. The zones of occupation in Germany, now including a French zone, all used the same postal stamps when Garrit arrived in Berlin. Then the Soviets issued one of their own. This seemed typical, because they were not making negotiations for a reunited Germany easy.

Negotiations for a united currency reform stalled, and when the *Deutsche Mark* was introduced by the three western allies since the Soviets refused, it was only a matter of days before the East German Mark was rolled out in 1948 and stamps were over-printed with the words Soviet Occupation Zone.

A letter dated 30th June 1948 didn't arrive until the third week in July. Izzy was getting used to this and understood, now, this was out of Garrit's control.

Mein liebes Mädchen,

At last I have work. I am using my languages again, so that is good. I have enough money to buy what I need, which is not much. Soon perhaps you can come to see me. I do miss you so. I hope Ester can come too, although life for her would not be easy here.

You remember I told you I was in a hostel. Well, guess what? I have my own apartment now, and it's not far from where I lived with Mama and Papa. It is in a block that is half new and half old but still in Prenzlauer Berg, so I am most fortunate. This is such a good area. Sometimes I take my lunch into the Weißensee cemetery. It is so quiet despite its vastness. I passed a young girl there the other day. She was sitting on a gravestone and her head hung down. She looked so sad, but I find peace there. I know Mama and Papa are far away somewhere else with no marker to visit. I have almost given up all hope of finding them and I'm coming to believe they perished with all the millions of others. I find it good for my soul to wander the long alleyways in the graveyard or sit under the trees that are ancient and will still be there after I, too, have gone. It is wild and unkempt after many years of abuse and neglect, but a small group are trying to restore it with proper reverence.

I miss you, Mein Liebling. Komm bald zu mir.

Soon? Yes, it must be soon, Izzy thought, *with or without Ester.*

CHAPTER 25

Yorkshire, 1975

Now that a planning application had been made, the petition to save the care home was gathering momentum. All the relatives of residents, the staff, and local wildlife groups were contacted. Will and Heather met with each of the people who lived in the houses to the rear of the gardens of the home and behind the spinney.

"Yes, I had a letter. I'm not happy to hear this," one man said. "The noise and disturbance of high-density housing will be terrible. Even if they are bigger family houses, I'm not happy. We bought this place specifically for the wildlife and quiet."

Another spoke at length about the loss of light that might be caused by houses to the rear of his property. "I have my art studio at the back of our garden. I'm not having houses blocking out my natural light."

"You are able to view the plans. We must gather detailed evidence where at all possible," Heather said. "Planning officers will take a very dim view of speculation and hearsay."

"Don't you worry, lass," the artist said. "I'll get my case together in fine detail. There's highway safety too. Have you thought of that? All these extra people using the lane for entrance and exit won't do. Even if they change that and take them out the other way, they'd all be turning out and clogging up the main road into town. That could be dangerous."

"Thanks, hadn't thought of that." Will wrote in his notebook.

Gradually their case was coming together. Will's solicitor friend knew someone who was a chartered surveyor, and he in turn knew someone who was a member of the Royal Town Planning Institute. He wanted payment for his advice, but after some discussion he was persuaded to give his opinion free of charge. The key to the whole plan was the spinney at the side and back of the home. Without that, access would be denied, and the project would not be viable.

More than three hundred objections flooded to the District Council from people concerned about the effects on the spinney as a local amenity and on wildlife.

Will did some research and started to seek tree preservation orders on the woodland to the rear of the home by writing to the local council. He discovered that the spinney was made from spoil banks from when the railways were built more than one hundred years ago. "It has historic value," he said to Heather.

One evening as they sat in the pub and pored over what they had gathered thus far, a loud laugh on the other side of the room caused them both to look up. The bar was teeming. A fug of smoke hung below the ceiling and the noise was becoming too much to bear.

"Let's go somewhere else," Heather said. "This is too noisy. It's hard to hear ourselves think."

"My mum's out this evening, and she said Stella was going too. They talked about going to see *Monty Python and the Holy Grail*."

"I read about that. It's supposed to be very funny. Where's it on?"

"They were going to make a day and night of it and go to Manchester on the train."

"That's a treat for Stella."

"She doesn't get out that much, so yes. There's a small guest house where they can have a room on the ground floor. They've stayed there before."

Heather looked at Will. "So, they're not coming back tonight."

"You'll be quite safe. Remember, I said … no etchings." He smiled and took her hand. "Promise I'll behave."

"Let's go, then." Heather stood.

Once they were through Will's front door, he tossed his keys onto the hall stand and turned to Heather. "I've been dying to tell you the latest," he said. "Last week, the District Council placed an emergency tree preservation order on the entire spinney. It's only for six months, but I gather it's highly likely it'll become permanent."

"Wow! That's amazing, Will. Well done." Heather flung her arms around him.

Will cleared his throat.

"Sorry," she said, stepping back.

"And," he continued, avoiding eye contact, "Yorkshire Wildlife Trust has also raised an objection to the development. They have a conservation officer, called Mark something-or-other, who said the spinney constitutes — what was it? Oh yes: 'local distinctiveness and a sense of place'." Will frowned as he spoke, remembering the quote from the wonderful Mark Something. "He went on to say there are lots of examples of green spaces managed by local communities, and this could be one option for the site. He said it's an important area which links Sites of Scientific Interest with the local park. Honestly, I had no idea." Will was smiling now, and Heather's breath escaped in a rush.

"My goodness, the big guns," she said with a wobble in her voice as she regarded the animation on his face.

"I think we may succeed here. If they withdrew their application for building, that would be the best result ever." Will led the way into the small sitting room.

"I think we should celebrate. Have you any beer or wine in the house?" Heather laughed up at him.

"There's usually a bottle of Blue Nun in the fridge. I'll have a beer. Which do you want?"

Once they were sitting at the table, Heather with her wine and Will with a bottle of John Smith's, they clinked glasses and he took a long drag of his beer. She watched his Adam's apple bobbing as he swallowed and experienced a tingle somewhere just below her navel. He looked at his bottle as he lowered it. "Ah! Not as good as the pub, but not bad. I've got a Party Seven in the cupboard, but that's probably a bit much." Then he realised she was staring. "What? What are you looking at? Have I froth on my chin?"

"No." She chuckled. "If you really want to know, I was thinking I'm sorry. I misjudged you very badly."

He shrugged and his mouth quirked up at one side. "It happens. And now?"

"Now? Now, I'd like to see your etchings." She smiled self-consciously at her daring.

He stood, came around to her side of the table, put out his hand, and pulled her to her feet. "I have no etchings, I told you that, but I could show you something else. If you're sure?" He smiled at her, his eyes deep.

She put back her head and stood on her toes, bringing her face so close to his she could smell the fruity, malty aroma from his beer. She liked it and leaned up to kiss him. It was brief and she pulled back. She was bursting with new-found confidence.

His arms came around her. She felt the firm warmth of them on her back and kissed him again, this time making it longer.

Her heart thudded. She hadn't experienced this before. Not with Kev, never with Brian. This was an epiphany. Something unique and complete. She was proud of herself. She revelled in her independence and power.

His tongue slipped between her lips and sought the tip of her own. His lips were dry and firm, and the kiss was long and perfect. Her hands slid around his backside and she pulled him to her, arching against him. She was conscious of his whole body, aware of every moulding and alert to his need for her.

"Yes?" he whispered. "Are you certain of this? I will show you what I have, but it won't be a single time, not for me."

She nodded and he took her hand. She followed him up to his bedroom. He didn't switch on any lights, but a soft amber glow crept in from the street, cocooning them in its warmth. She was safe here, she was certain. More so than ever before.

Will was gentle, ensuring it was all about her, touching her hair, her cheek. He kissed her shoulder and slowly moved up her neck before nibbling her ear. He turned her, so her back was to him, and his arms came around and caressed her breasts. He undid her clothing with a little fumbling, but she liked that. He wasn't so experienced, then. Turning her again he stared into her eyes, asking for reassurance, perhaps, before holding her face, tilting his head and gently lowering his lips to hers. Her heart beat faster. Then her blouse and bra slipped off her shoulders to the floor and she began to unbutton his shirt. He gave her a light, teasing kiss between each one, her anticipation increasing as his skin was exposed. She brushed her hands across his naked chest.

The act itself came quickly. Neither of them could wait longer. Heather groaned as he entered her, and her legs came around him to keep him close. Never had the act of love been so loving. She relished his attention and his wish to ensure it was the best it could be for her.

As they lay peacefully afterwards, he said, "You know I love you, don't you? I have for a long time. I told you this was not a one time thing for me, and I meant it."

At that moment, sheer joy pulsed through Heather. No one had ever treated her this way before. Kev was always about his own gratification. Brian lacked imagination for her needs. This man had ensured she had not only enjoyed what they had just done but had shown her that she mattered, that she was important to him. Now he had said he loved her. He hadn't got her into his bed for his needs alone.

I've heard all that before, she thought. *Undying love ... oh, and by the way, let me into your knickers. Yes, this is very different ... isn't it?*

CHAPTER 26

England, 1948

Garrit had given up expecting to find definitive news of his parents. He had certainly stopped actively searching. His surprise when a communication arrived, suggesting his mother was in an internment camp in Bavaria, was immense. He had to sit down and get his breath. Then he doubted it could be true. Surely this must be some other woman, perhaps with the same name. In his letter to Izzy, he tried to describe how he was feeling about the news but found it impossible.

Izzy had read that it might be possible that it was indeed Garrit's mother, as millions of people had been displaced after the end of the war. There was no news of his father, but Garrit was expecting to travel to Föhrenwald to the displaced persons' camp very soon. When Izzy told Ester, her eyes shone with feverish brilliance.

"Oh, my goodness. Garrit must be so excited at this possibility. I do wish I was there with him. Surely, we will go soon. I'm so much better, aren't I?"

Weakened by her pneumonia, in a chilly summer of 1948, Izzy sat by her bed for hours, gently stroking her forehead as her breathing became laboured again. Her normally bright approach to all things was dimmed by her illness. Her face was pale and her lips grey in the fading light of the evening. Izzy sat in silence as her patient dozed fitfully. Ester remained calm. Instead of raging against her fate, she thought of those around her and of her family, now so distant.

"Dearest Izzy. What would we have done without you? What I'm most sorry about is not seeing Mama again. Garrit will care for her, I know. I will be joining Papa, I think. I'm not frightened." Even Ester's voice was serene.

Izzy fought back her tears, but her throat constricted.

"Don't be sad for me, Izzy. You don't need me. You have your own strength. Go to Garrit. Tell him I am happy. Don't let him suffer or feel needlessly guilty."

Ester's death hit them all. Her fragile little heart, so stout in many other ways, could not stand the onslaught and she finally passed away with Izzy at her bedside. After she breathed her last shallow breath, Izzy stood and gazed out at the grey landscape of the garden. The colours seemed a faded memory after so much hardship and suffering. This was utterly unfair. Izzy banged her hand against the window frame. Ester had always been so brave, uncomplaining, good at seeing the positives in everything around her when others, who had so much more, could not. Just when better news was on the horizon for her and Garrit, this had been sent to tear away all hope.

When the cold had finally left, rain which could not sink into the frozen ground, meltwater from snowdrifts, and a particularly high tide brought further devastation across the country.

The Strong family stood in a small huddle in the cemetery under dripping trees, shivering under umbrellas. Ideally Ester would have been buried with Jewish rites, but that was impossible with present conditions. They all agreed, including Garrit from afar, that it was better she be laid to rest with dignity and respect rather than waiting for the correct circumstances. As it was, the grave itself was almost impossible for the men to dig. Water kept seeping into it, and so everything was delayed. Garrit did not have the money to travel and when he wrote to Izzy, his letter was full of heartbreak, guilt and sadness, which added to her own.

Floods in the southeast were particularly bad and trainlines across England were again affected, meaning travel was impossible. The country was left with huge bills for reparation and many people were displaced for months while their homes were made habitable after flooding. The people of Izzy's town and the school were luckier than many, but she was frustrated at her inability to travel to be at Garrit's side. The years since his departure had been long and hard. How she longed to have his arms around her and to be able to comfort him in his despair.

Her opportunity came in early 1949, despite the deteriorating relations between the allied forces of East and West.

"Ah, Izzy, is this wise?" her papa asked over breakfast one morning.

"Probably not, but I must go. I must give Garrit the chain that Ester left for him. He is desperate to know the details of Ester's passing and although I have written, of course, it's not the same."

"We shall miss you, Izzy," Rose said later that day. "The news from Germany, and Berlin in particular, is not good. I shall worry about you until you return."

Izzy managed to find a travel agent in Manchester who liaised with a bureau in the allied sector of West Berlin, and her boat and train travel was arranged. She was shocked at the expense, but Papa agreed for her to go.

"I'm an old man. It will be yours when I go, so if you need it now, you shall have it. I shall make it right with your sisters."

"Papa, I cannot thank you enough."

"You deserve it, child. Rose went to Oxford University; Delphi went to Australia. You visited Germany before the war, I know, but you have more than earned this since then. Go. Make your peace over there and come back to us happier than you clearly are right now."

Tears threatened, but she managed to withhold them as her cheek rubbed against the tweed of her father's jacket when she hugged him.

It was a seemingly endless and tiring journey. The boat train was only a little late, and the Channel was calm, thank goodness. The carriage Izzy was in rumbled across France and into Germany in its own slow and halting time. Her packet of sandwiches in their brown greaseproof paper only lasted across France, but she managed to buy something to keep her going and a cup of strong coffee at one of the station stopovers.

There was a long halt at the Soviet sector border, where her papers were checked by a stern army official with a dog. He took his time, all the while glancing at Izzy then back to her passport and other travel documents. There was a lot of clanking and shunting as the engine was changed and shouting as one crew left and different men took over. Another official came along the carriage, and again her papers were scrutinised. She tried hard to breathe normally and look him in the eye. After more halts and holdups, she alighted in Berlin in the middle of the afternoon.

She was shocked. Along the route she had seen evidence of destruction, but it was nothing compared to here. The city was unrecognisable as the place in which she had flirted, danced and dined before the war.

On one side of the street, a building stood undisturbed. Directly opposite, a pile of rubble and a skeletal façade stood with broken drainpipes and half a fireplace exposed to the air. A shredded piece of fabric blew in the breeze from an upstairs window that contained no glass. A group of women were clearing rubble by filling a basket and struggling across the devastation with it between them. They were covered in a grey film of dust, and they wore thick socks and large boots which emphasised their thin legs. The *trümmerfrau*, Izzy guessed. By all accounts there were hundreds of such groups doing this job, across the city and beyond.

She saw a man pinning a poster to a wall. His raincoat looked shabby and his homburg hat was pulled low over his eyes. He looked over his shoulder before hastening away, and when she looked it said *Boycott gegen Terror*. She knew there was censorship of press in the East. Was this a sign of things to come? Incongruously she saw a man riding a bicycle with a basket on the front. A blanket covered something and then she spotted the pink snout of a piglet, before the blanket was hastily replaced and the man wobbled on his way.

As she wandered along the street towards her hotel, she stood for a moment and watched a man and two women looking at a board covered in papers and white cards. When she stepped closer, she saw they were all job offers, mainly in reconstruction. This must be what kept unemployment at a low level.

Izzy found her hotel. It was small, and her room was tiny but clean enough. The wallpaper had seen better days. It was tinged brown and smelled of cigarettes. She sat and tested the bed. It was narrow and the mattress thin. The bed covering was thick and full of air and feathers. So different to the blankets and eiderdown at home; this was the *Bettdeckung* that she remembered, and it suddenly made the room more familiar and friendly. Still, it was only for one night.

The landlady showed her the bathroom at the end of the corridor and left her to settle down for the night. Tomorrow, Garrit would come to collect her. Today he was working, and tonight she would recover from the awful journey. She had been tempted to ask him to come this evening, but she wasn't sure of what would greet her on her arrival, so this is what she had arranged. It was a long while since they had been together, and much had changed for them both. Now she regretted her reticence, but she would survive one more night alone.

She hardly slept. The noise from the street, the unfamiliar odours of her accommodation, and her anticipation all kept her awake.

The next morning, Izzy stood just inside the hotel's front door, peering up and down the path but only able to see a limited distance. Standing outside on the street in this changed city might be asking for trouble that she did not think she was capable of handling. She looked at her wristwatch yet again. She was early, of course. Staying in her room to wait was not an option. She left her small brown suitcase against the wall and opened the door to scan the busy street outside before looking again at the time and ducking back indoors.

She turned to the landlady. "*Entschuldigung, darf ich ein Glas Wasser haben, bitte?*" Izzy's throat was parched. The hard brown bread and the poor excuse for coffee at breakfast time had done nothing to ease her thirst.

The landlady sighed and came back a moment later with the water in a calcium-stained glass.

Izzy took a reluctant sip.

"Izzy!" He had come in behind her, breathless, when she wasn't even looking.

"Oh!" She closed her eyes. Her heart thumped. When she opened them, Garrit still stood before her. Without another word, she stepped into his arms.

CHAPTER 27

Yorkshire, 1975

On Monday, after more than five hundred objections had been logged, the owners of the land upon which the spinney and the care home sat withdrew their application. It also transpired that the small area of woodland was featured in the council's local plan as an area of 'Nature Conservation Interest'. The owners declined to comment to the local press about what might happen next, but the building of houses was not an option. Will and Heather's work had saved The Beeches from annihilation.

Will's next move was to request that the little woodland be offered as a local community trust or wildlife association. In this way, it could be protected for future generations. He awaited the council's response, but was hopeful a committee could start to act.

There was much rejoicing all around, with a small party at the care home to celebrate.

"I'm so proud of you," Heather said to Will. "This might not have been possible without all your work."

"And you've given me the support to get it done. We make a great team."

Heather basked in his praise. She was unused to receiving such from anyone. "I think I've always been a bit of a duffer," she said. "I do think I'm getting better at things, though. I'm much more confident than I used to be. That's down to Izzy and especially you."

"Oh, my darling girl, you are one of the brightest, bravest people, I know." Will kissed her lightly.

He *was* great for her confidence, and she was aware that it grew daily through being with him. As the weeks passed, Heather remained happy, both with her work and with him. Her belief in herself increased all the time.

Later that week, Heather and Will lay together in bed, sated and content. Heather's mum had gone to the cinema with a friend and wouldn't be home until eleven.

"I finished my painting of Stella this afternoon." Will stroked her tummy, making Heather giggle and writhe.

"That tickles."

"Sorry. I wondered, would you come home with me tomorrow and give it to her? I'm a bit nervous for some stupid reason. I do so want her to like it."

"It's fab. How could she not? It's such a great likeness but more than that, you have your own unique style. I absolutely love it."

"You're biased."

"No! Well, maybe, but it is incredibly good. You're wasted as a caretaker in an old people's home."

"It suits me well enough."

"You could do so much more with your talent and brains. Look at how you managed to save the care home, and the committee looking after the spinney is all down to you."

"Down to us. Anyway, I'm happy. Leave it. Come here and kiss me again." He pulled her closer and when he nuzzled her neck, she forgot what she'd been about to say.

"I have something for you, Stells," Will said the next day, turning sideways to enter the living room with the picture wrapped loosely in an old sheet covered with paint splodges.

"Hello, loves," his mum, Debra, said to them. She wound up her ball of blue wool and stuck her needles into it before putting down her knitting on a little side table. "Ee, this pattern's complicated," she said. "Goodness, what have you got there?"

"We-ell," Will started and then paused, looking around. Stella wasn't in the room.

"Go on, Will. Show her." Heather nudged him. "He's been so busy in his spare time, what with the petition to save the home and with this, too. This is special. You have one skilful, clever son, here."

"Oh, I know, Heather. What's he got for us this time?"

Will propped the painting across the arms of a chair and carefully took off the cloth. "The paint's still not quite hardened." He stood back.

"My word," Debra said. "It's like she's in the room with us. That's amazing."

"Where is she, Mum?"

"She's lying down, love. Can you take this up to show her? She's not been feeling too good. That awful hacking cough is no better. You were in late last night and gone this morning before she woke up. I was going to ask if you thought we should make a doctor's appointment. Get him out to the house, even. Do take this up, love. It will cheer her no end. It's so good."

Will gathered up the painting and went towards the door. He turned to Heather.

"No," she said. "You go. I'll wait here. This is your moment." She turned to Debra as he left the room. "He's so talented."

"He came second in his year at art college. Got a distinction." She picked up her knitting again.

"I didn't know."

"He's modest, too." She smiled at Heather and touched her hand. "We're lucky to have him, aren't we?"

"We certainly are. It's such a shame he can't use his art skills more. He could earn a living, I'm sure."

"He's all right. It suits us all," Debra said, echoing her son's words from the night before.

Heather heard him pounding down the stairs at that point, bringing an end to the conversation.

"Mum, she's burning up, but shivering. I think we should call the doctor now." He glanced at his watch. "I might just get the end of surgery." He crossed the room with a few strides and lifted the receiver. He held it between his ear and his shoulder and picked up a piece of paper tucked under the phone. As he looked at it, he pulled the dial around with his finger. The whirring as it returned, ready for the next number, was loud in the silence of the room.

"I'll pop upstairs," his mum whispered to Heather, who nodded her reply.

"He'll come after surgery. Well, you heard me say how concerned I am, and he knows her well, of course," Will said.

"You look worried. Is she very poorly?"

"I think she is."

"I can see myself home," Heather said.

"Don't go. Please?" Will put his head on one side. "I need you."

Heather felt a tingle of joy but squashed it down. How terrible to feel so happy when Stella was so poorly, and Will was on edge.

The doctor's prognosis was serious. "She has pneumonia, I'm afraid."

Heather gasped. Abruptly she remembered the experiences Izzy had shared with her. Garrit's sister had died of just this. The others in the room looked at her, but she managed to say nothing.

The doctor continued, "I think you've caught it in good time, but we'll call for an ambulance to be on the safe side, as she's already vulnerable."

Will and Debra were to accompany Stella to the hospital. Heather dithered about whether to stay or go until Will said, "Please stay. I'll come home as soon as she's settled in. Mum will want to wait with her while they find her a ward bed, I'm sure."

Stella looked small and frail, dwarfed by the ambulance trolley. Its red cellular blanket sucked all the colour from her face as they wheeled her out of the front door. She gave a wan smile as she passed Heather, who stood in the living room doorway.

"So sorry," the young girl whispered as she passed. "Look after Will, won't you?"

Heather closed the door after watching them trail down the front path behind the ambulance men. All she could do was wait. Trepidation made it impossible to settle. She went into the kitchen and made herself a cup of tea. She switched on the television and stood by it as she watched it warm up. An episode of *The Sweeney* came to life, but it was too noisy. BBC1 had *Angels*, but she quickly turned that over. The last thing she needed was a hospital drama.

It was very late when Heather heard Will's key in the door. She rubbed her eyes and hurried out into the hall.

"They've got her on intravenous antibiotics and oxygen. They say she'll be fine, but we'll know more tomorrow. They've let Mum stay. It's not visiting, obviously, but they took pity on her when she pleaded with them and swore she wouldn't get in the way. She's beside the bed in a chair. She'll be knackered tomorrow." He put his arms out and Heather entered his embrace. "Would you make coffee if I have a quick bath?"

"Of course," Heather said. "What about something to eat? She'll be all right, you know."

"I love your positivity. No, just a drink." Will kissed her forehead and she watched him drag himself upstairs, leaning on the banister as he went, his legs heavy.

Half an hour later, they sat together on the sofa. "What's the latest on the Izzy story? Talk to me about something different," Will said as he sipped his coffee. "Take my mind away from the hospital."

Heather blinked and swallowed. She couldn't possibly tell him about Ester. She took a sip of her drink to give herself some thinking time. "Izzy's such an incredible lady. She went to Germany to see Garrit in 1949. It must have been such a strange experience — everything bombed and broken, people trying to survive, trying to find relatives."

"Did he find his parents, this Garrit fella?"

"Well, that's the thing. That year, they had news that his mother was in a camp in Bavaria. There seemed to have been no news of his father. By that time, apparently, there were only a couple of such places left, and they were vast. Five or six thousand people in each."

"But did he find them?"

CHAPTER 28

Germany, 1949

Izzy accompanied Garrit to Föhrenwald. The journey, under normal circumstances, should have taken only one day since it was not far from München. Everything was paperwork, paperwork. Travel documents had to be obtained, and these were checked as they left the Soviet sector in Berlin and then several times after that, too. They managed to get rail transport at first, but it stopped and re-started a thousand times, or so it seemed. They had to change trains more than once, and at Nürnberg the station was undergoing significant rebuilding. There was no accommodation to be found anywhere. Like in every other large centre, there was major devastation with buildings crumbling and vast piles of rubble everywhere. Façades with no windows rose into the sky.

Izzy and Garrit stayed on a platform, huddled together in a corner and dozing only fitfully. It was draughty, dirty and noisy.

"This is horrendous," Izzy said.

"Better than that room." Garrit nodded at the dirty door of the small waiting room that had somehow survived the bombs, or perhaps it was a corner temporarily reinstated for the purpose. "It smelled of stale urine. I couldn't let you in there."

"I can't believe our beloved Germany has been wasted like this. The bombed-out shells of peoples' lives are bad enough. The food shortages are appalling. How on earth do you stay sane?" It had been a week since Izzy had arrived in Berlin and she still could not bear to see the ruins and the desolate people standing in line for whatever they could get.

Garrit shrugged and gave her his gentle smile. "We queue. We shiver. We endure, because what else can we do? When the sun sparkles on a shard of broken glass or a shadow of a tree falls across the grass in front of where I stand, I am happy. Sometimes I wonder if it's awful to feel such joy. Life continues."

"I saw a pregnant woman yesterday. She had a toddler trailing along beside her. Both had clothes that looked shabby and ill-fitting. The little girl's dress hung below her coat, clearly too big for her, and she was grubby with dust. Her hair was tangled. But as I watched, she looked up at her mother and giggled about something. Mmm, life goes on," Izzy said.

"And people are thankful for many things," Garrit added. "I'm lucky. I have you, I have this journey and perhaps I shall find my mother. The sun shone yesterday. A train will come soon. That old lady gave us an egg each for our breakfast before we left."

Later, they walked and then cadged a lift on the back of a farm cart. Izzy must have slept with the swaying motion, because she awoke when the farm labourer stopped the plodding horse and shouted for them to get off because he was going no further. The last part of the journey was again on foot. They made their way together, their hands joined.

As they neared their destination it was late, and the sun was blindingly brilliant as it sank low in the sky. Garrit looked at Izzy. Laughing, he pulled her from the road into the woods that lined it. As they went deeper, it was strangely calm. Birds sang but were not to be seen. Their steps were muffled by the thick layer of leaves. The sun slanted between the bows and stippled the ground, freckling the ancient trunks and highlighting the leaves like a painting. A squirrel flicked its tail and leapt away from them, springing along the branches and quickly disappearing.

Garrit turned to Izzy and stroked her hair from her face. "I think we must rest here for the night. Can you bear it?"

Later, as they lay on his coat after sharing the last of the stale bread they had been able to buy, Garrit said, "Let's believe this is the Kaiserhof. Do you remember those chandeliers? Well, look up. Do you see something to rival those lights? The stars are bright tonight and there are a thousand million. The roots of the trees delve deep and form strong foundations. The walls are clothed in greens and browns of every soft hue. Listen to the sounds."

Izzy did as he asked. The orchestra of the forest filled her head. The soft flutter of leaves whispered their songs to the breeze; unseen movement of little mammals kept rhythm; the quiet creaking of ancient bows waved their twigs like batons keeping the time of the music. All soothed her spirit and as she lay her head on his chest, she could hear his heartbeat too. Gone were the ruins and desolation. The grubby austerity of shortages and queues were driven away. She could almost believe she was back at the elegant hotel Kaiserhof, sipping her coffee and smiling at her companions.

The corners of her mouth tweaked now, and she looked up at Garrit. His head came to hers, and he kissed her.

"Your hair smells of the farmer's straw from that cart," he said.

"I may smell worse before the journey is done. That cold tap water in the toilets at the last station was a while ago."

He laughed and rolled over her. "Do I care? Not a jot." He leaned down to kiss her again, pinning her hands either side of her head. His lips met hers with greater fervency.

They made love under the stars. The cold didn't matter. There was no worry about the noises they both made. They laughed and rolled and finally, sated, they slept.

CHAPTER 29

When Izzy awoke, Garrit was sitting with his back against a tree trunk, watching her. His coat was over her. He smiled. "You have leaves in your hair."

"How long have you been awake? What time is it?"

He looked at his watch. "It's just after seven. Come on, lazy girl. There's a stream about half a kilometre away. You can have a splash wash before we leave here. You better drag a comb through that mop, too. If we get to Föhrenwald looking like this, they may lock us up."

As Izzy and Garrit approached the small town, he took hold of her hand again. "I find I am nervous," he said, giving a small self-deprecating laugh. "I'm not sure what to expect. I have those awful images in my head of Auschwitz and Buchenwald which were described on the news."

"They were two of the six death camps. There were literally thousands of other camps, but this is not going to be like those two. This is being run by the Americans, and it's been here for years." Izzy stopped walking and put her hand to the side of Garrit's face, turning his head and gazing into his dark eyes. "Whatever we find, we find it together," she said. "We will face this as we have faced everything else."

He rested his forehead against hers for a moment, and his soft breath caressed her. Then he nodded and they continued towards the town. As they came close, they realised this was different to those images that had become everyone's worst nightmare.

Identical small buildings lined the streets, which were all named after American states. They walked up Pennsylvania

Strasse and, after asking once or twice, managed to find the main administrative block. After a long wait and a lot of paperwork, they finally met someone who could help. An officer in American uniform invited them to sit. "Coffee?" He crossed to a pot sitting on a hotplate atop a filing cabinet.

They had not tasted anything like it for years. Izzy watched as Garrit sipped his, savouring every mouthful. She smiled to herself at the look on his face as she enfolded her own cup with her fingers to warm them.

The officer went to a cabinet and found a brown manilla file, which he tossed onto his desk. Unwinding the string that held it shut, he opened it and sat saying nothing for a while as he read the contents. Izzy waited and watched as Garrit fidgeted with impatience. The aroma of the hot drink was powerful, and Izzy's stomach started grumbling. She had eaten next to nothing recently.

"Yes, we have a Frau Shain. Frau Hannah Ester Shain. Do you think that's who you're after? Her date of birth is June 1886," the man opposite them said.

Garrit let his breath out and leaned forwards in his chair. He grabbed Izzy's hand.

The officer continued speaking as he looked at his papers. "She was in Mechelen transit camp in Belgium and then Herzogenbusch in the Netherlands for a while. After that it was Neuengamme, well one of the subcamps up there in the north. It was a labour camp, and she was involved in brickmaking. In 1940 Himmler visited and declared it to be inefficient so a new brick works was built, and prisoners were involved in construction work in Hamburg. It was brutal at times. She just missed the death marches from the subcamps there. Lots of the unlucky ones were marched to Bergen-Belson and Osnabrück. She was transferred to Malchow, which was savage under the SS wardress by the name of Luise Danz. *She* got what she deserved. Hannah Shain came to us from Malchow suffering from exhaustion and malnutrition. Fortunately, we won the goddam war.

"Okay, you guys. I can have Frau Shain brought here. Probably best. One of my people will go and find her." He picked up the phone on his desk and spoke briefly into the heavy black receiver before replacing it on its cradle with a clunk. "She's living on Indiana Strasse. A little warning. People are changed. She will look and act differently from when you last knew her. Try not to let your expression show when you first meet her. Don't throw yourselves at her. Let her take in what she sees and hears. Give her time. You may even find she wants to stay here, although that's not a long-term option. These places are closing. We are one of the last two. We need these folks to find their homes and relatives."

"What has her life been like here?" Garrit asked.

Izzy sat on the edge of her chair. She was as anxious as Garrit by this time. She glanced at his face. Worry was etched there. His body was tense; she could tell by the angle of his shoulders and head. Her own heart was pounding faster, and she was breathless. This woman, his mother, had not wanted her to be with her son when they had last met, but so much had changed since then. She prayed that her circumstances would mean she was understanding of all the hardships they too had suffered, even though they were not a match for hers.

"It's not easy. We often have twenty-five to a room and people sharing bunks. Food is desperately short. We had no water for five days a while back."

Then they heard footsteps and voices approaching. Izzy gripped the wooden arms of her chair and tried to calm herself.

She must school her face to be neutral. She must not be shocked at what she saw. She must…

The door opened. Garrit grasped Izzy's arm. His chair scraped back with a screech and she jumped. He stood slowly and she turned. There stood a small, thin, grey-haired woman of indeterminate age, her skin nut-brown and lined. Gone was the sophisticated lady of a pre-war era with smart timeless fashion and elegant poise, but her brown eyes were unmistakeable. Here stood a woman in an ill-fitting chestnut-coloured skirt with a drooping hemline. Her woollen top was brown, and she wore flat shoes, but this was Frau Shain, Garrit's mother.

In silence, Garrit and she moved towards each other. "*Mutter*," he murmured.

"*Mein Sohn, mein lieber Junge*," she said. "I never thought this day would come." Tears sparkled on her eyelashes but none fell as she took hold of his hands. As she did so her sleeves rose up, exposing thin, bony wrists. Garrit dropped her hands and enfolded her slight form in his arms, and they stood saying nothing as they held each other. After a moment, Izzy saw tears seeping down his rough cheek.

Then Hannah pulled back, stroked the side of his head and looked at Izzy. "Izzy, is this you? After all these years. I would know you anywhere." Then a small frown appeared. "And Ester? Where is your sister, Garrit?"

"Oh, *Mutti*," he said, addressing her in the childish way of those long-ago years. He hung his head.

Izzy got to her feet and hurried across the room, putting her arm around them both as best she could and resting her forehead against the side of Hannah's head, despite what the American officer had advised. "She got pneumonia. Her body was already frail and was weakened further by the dreadful winter weather of 1946 and '47. I was with her in England. She had such a wonderful, gentle soul and she was brave throughout. At the end she was calm."

"Were you not there, my dearest boy?" Hannah looked up at Garrit.

"I had returned to Germany, to Berlin. I wanted to find you and Papa. She was to follow when I had somewhere to live. It wasn't to be."

"No, there is much that was not to be," Hannah said softly.

The American soldier, who had sat at his desk in silence throughout this exchange, stood. "Why don't you folks go through there?" He indicated a door in the far wall. "We've got it laid out like a living room with a couch an' all. There's a small bathroom too. I'll bring through some coffee. You've all got a deal of catching up to do."

They took his advice and were grateful for it. Hannah chose to sit on the edge of an easy chair while Garrit and Izzy were left with the sofa. There was an awkward silence until the soldier came in with a tray. The activities associated with passing cups and organising themselves was a blessed relief. None of them knew where to start.

Izzy broke the constraint with what she hoped was a non-contentious question. "What do you do here, Hannah?"

Hannah gave a small smile. "Some say we are still prisoners, even though we are free. Life is not always easy. Some of the soldiers are antisemitic and some of us have been persecuted, even here." She shrugged. "I am lucky to have been brought to Föhrenwald. We have a good community here. All the row houses were built for employees at the I.G. Farben munitions works originally. In 1938." It was strange to hear her use the American term for the terraces of dwellings. "There were many nationalities here before I came, but President Eisenhower has decreed it is for Jewish people only, now. We worship as we please. There is a strong Hasidic influence here to our religion. It's very conservative in its practices, but who can blame us after... Anyway, it's not obligatory, and we all jog along together very nicely. The director is a very young man, but he encouraged us to have a school here for our children and there is training for the young men. There are doctors here who are Hungarian." Hannah smiled.

"Do you have enough to eat?" Garrit frowned.

Hannah raised her eyes. "Food has become much more rationed. We have had some of the GI dried and canned food to keep us going. I am used to eating little. We all are. No, there is not enough. For the children it is very hard." Then she spoke in a whisper. "The butchers in the basements help."

Izzy shook her head and frowned. "Sorry?"

"It is the Black Market. Poor Henry Cohen. He's the director here, but he's only in his twenties. He tries to put a stop to it. He makes unannounced visits. The butchers in the basements are carving up meat." She laughed and her skinny shoulders shook. Now she had started talking, she couldn't seem to stop. "But here it is like a Shabbat meal every day compared with before. There, we were kept alive so we could work. We might have had a tiny piece of sausage or some margarine to go with our small piece of black bread, but not often. Sometimes we had hot water with vegetable peelings in. When we couldn't survive, there were hundreds, thousands more replacements. I took bread from a dead girl one evening. I hid it in my clothing overnight to have in the morning. She didn't need it." She shrugged again and shook her head, as if wiping that from her mind. "There is talk of difficulties in Berlin, I hear."

"In the West it is almost impossible. In the East the Soviets are seeing us right. They are angry about the West's introduction of the *Deutsche Mark*, though, and are threatening to blockade all access to the sectors under Western control. Food is already scarce there, and people are starving."

"Berlin is like a little island in the middle of the Soviet sector. The Western allies have always assumed the goodwill of the East to allow them access," Izzy said, "but I think it's falling apart."

"You follow what is going on there?" Garrit asked.

"Oh yes," Hannah said. "We are free here. We have our own newspaper. It's called *Bamidbar*." She looked at Izzy. "That means *The Desert*."

Izzy nodded.

"And we have radio. I like it here." She sighed. "I know I cannot stay forever, though. And anyway, after the dreadful tuberculosis epidemic last year, I know it's not always safe to be enclosed and living on top of each other as we do. That time I was lucky. It seems I am charmed many times over."

Garrit shifted in his seat and glanced at Izzy. He cleared his throat and shuffled again.

"Say it, son. Ask it," Hannah said.

"Will you return with us to Berlin? I have a place to live and I earn money. It's small and shabby, but we would be together again."

"In truth, I am happy here, but as I say, I know I cannot stay forever. It's a camp for displaced people, and I am on my own. I must leave at some point. I'm so happy you've found me. I didn't believe it would happen. I thought perhaps you had made a new life in England. I was grateful that you had left when you did. It kept me going, that thought. Yes, I will come. It will take some time to organise. I shall have to start all that."

"I haven't asked you about Papa," Garrit said, avoiding his mother's gaze, which was fixed upon him as if she couldn't believe what she saw.

"He is gone. I know it. I had word from the authorities, but I knew of it before. I sensed it in my soul."

Garrit slid off the sofa and knelt before her. He took her hands.

"He was a target, you see. He was a doctor and too outspoken. We were separated when we were thrust out of those cattle wagons. All the men were taken. I turned and saw him being shoved with a rifle butt and he fell. I started to go to him but a woman next to me grabbed my arm and said, 'No, walk.' She probably saved my life. Then he was dragged up by his arm. I heard later that he had died. When tuberculosis and typhus were rife in the camp, the Nazis were desperate and ordered all the qualified medical personnel to nurse the sick. He spent his life healing and helping, but when he was ill there was no one to help him. Typhus, I think." She touched Garrit's head as he bowed it in her lap and his shoulders shuddered.

Izzy watched in silence as Hannah stared straight ahead. Still she had not cried. Perhaps she had shed all her tears in the past, or perhaps she needed to shut the door on that part of her heart, in order to survive.

Saying goodbye to Hannah, albeit temporarily, was an impossibly difficult moment. Garrit and Hannah clung to one another until they had to go. Izzy and Garrit returned to his apartment in Berlin after a long, arduous and grimy journey. Her time in Berlin was almost done, and her heart clenched each time she thought about her departure to England.

"I wish you could come, too," she said as they lay beside each other in his narrow bed.

"Perhaps when *Mutti* is here, we will both come. We could marry, and I could become a citizen of England. I would live anywhere with you."

Izzy looked up from her place on his chest. "Oh yes. That would be perfect. As soon as I get back, I'll investigate it. I'll find out what papers we need. Make sure you bring all your documents with you. Papa will help. Rose and Michael would offer support, too. Maybe even a proper place of employment."

Garrit shifted in the bed and returned her kiss with uninhibited passion. She rolled against the length of his body, aware of his excitement as she wriggled in closer. The future suddenly seemed less bleak. In fact, it had a rosy glow. The narrow bed, the peeling wallpaper, the creaky floorboards, the water-stained fabric at the windows all receded. They made love as if it was the first and last time.

Izzy resolutely squashed down the apprehension that it might be difficult to get permission for his mother. Perhaps he would come anyway. He could return here to visit. She stretched up and kissed him. Warmth spread through her. Perhaps all would come right in the end, and all these years of hardship and restraint would be forgotten.

CHAPTER 30

Yorkshire, 1975

There was a lot to celebrate that New Year's Eve. Not only was Stella home and recovered, but Heather and Will had cemented their relationship. She was more confident than she had been in her entire life, and all because he believed in her and complemented her in all ways.

Will was busy tidying the living room while Debra was in the kitchen with the two girls. Stella was threading cubes of cheese and pineapple onto cocktail sticks before pushing the points into a large potato covered in foil. Heather turned to open the bags of crisps. "3p," she commented. "They've gone up. Still, I s'pose it's an extra big bag." Then she opened the cheese straws and twiglets before poking around in the cupboard to find a suitable dish in which to put them. She was comfortable here with Will's family. It was her second home these days.

There was a quiche Lorraine in the oven and the vol-au-vent cases were already cooked and waiting to be filled. Heather's mum had made a cheesecake and was bringing that along with the rest of the Christmas cake she had baked back at the beginning of November. Some friends of Will were dropping into the party too. It promised to be a fun evening.

Will came in and said, "Right, the living room's done. What next?"

"There'll be a cloth in the airing cupboard, love. Put that on the sideboard and we can lay the drinks and glasses on there. That Party Seven will come in useful now, and there's a bottle of Blue Nun and that Rosé, the one in the funny shaped bottle with the straw base. They're in the fridge. Oh, and don't forget the bottle opener for the Rosé."

"I read that these nuns on the label had brown habits originally, and a printing error turned them blue," Will said as he looked at the bottle he had found.

"It was created by a German Jew," Heather added. "It's so popular. Seems appropriate somehow, after what I've learned from Izzy."

The little party went with a swing. The younger generation had a game of Twister while the parents and their friends looked on, laughed and shouted out suggestions.

"Put your right hand on the red circle. No, that's your left hand, I said right hand."

"Try your foot on the green one."

"The other green one. No? Well, try the yellow, then."

When Will collapsed on the mat at the end of the third round, they all gave up, exhausted.

The food vanished with speed, there was much laughing and joking, and a toast was made to Stella. They were all so pleased she was recovered and among them again. She blushed and hid her face in her hands, her vibrant red hair falling forwards. When the chimes of Big Ben rang out from the transistor radio, everyone gave everyone else a quick peck on the cheek, but Will took Heather in his arms and gave her a long kiss in front of everyone, which caused much hilarity, before he whispered 'Happy New Year' in her ear.

Will had walked Heather and her mum home, as everyone else was leaving his house. Now June had gone to bed, and the lovers sat together on the sofa. The door was shut, and they were both pleasantly snuggled and slightly tipsy. Heather said, "Shall we have another drink?"

"Not for me. I don't want a thick head tomorrow."

"Perhaps I'll have just a small glass of wine."

"Really? Your choice." He shrugged and kissed her before she arose to fetch it.

"What's your resolution for the New Year?" Heather asked Will when she returned.

"I don't know. Be happy. Enjoy my work. Make love to you." He kissed her with warm, soft lips that ensured her arousal.

She laughed and took a glug from her glass. Then she turned and knelt either side of his lap with her hands against the back of the sofa at each side of his head as she bent to kiss him again.

"Heather, what about your mum?"

"There's no way she'll be down."

"You're certainly Young Miss Confidence these days."

One thing led to another. She undid his belt. He unbuttoned her blouse.

As she sank down onto him, she gave a quiet moan and he echoed her.

Satisfied at last, she said, "Well, that's one part of the resolution. Now, what about work?" She giggled.

"What about work?" He stood to straighten himself, then bent to kiss the top of her head as she slumped on the sofa.

"Time to move up, surely. You can't be a caretaker all your life. What about your art? You could really go places."

"I'm happy at the care home. It suits us all."

"Yes, but you could manage an arts centre or open your own gallery."

"I must go," he said. "You're tipsy, talking nonsense and I've work tomorrow."

"Okay." She frowned. "There you are, then. Proving my point. If you were your own boss, you could take tomorrow off."

"Leave it, Heather. Thanks for making this evening so great. I'll see myself out. You look ready for sleep. Love you." He kissed her and left the room. She heard the front door click. *Hmm. That was a bit hasty*, she thought. *I only said what's true.* As she stood, she wobbled. *Ooh, more wine than I thought. Never done that before.* She giggled.

Heather had New Year's Day off, which was just as well as she slept late and had a stonking headache when she awoke.

"Morning," June said when she finally staggered down to the kitchen, feeling like death warmed up.

"Don't be so loud and cheery. My head's thumping."

"Have a large glass of water as well as a cup of tea. Wine dehydrates."

"I know, but it was fun at the time. Where's Friday's paper? I wanted to have a look at the job ads."

"You're not changing, are you? I thought you liked it at the care home. They certainly seem to like you, from what I hear."

"Oh no, not me. I love it, and I couldn't leave Izzy now. Do you know, Mum, I think she treats me a bit like her family, the child she never had. She doesn't have anyone else, now. I know we're not supposed to get too close, but she's so lovely and she's been so brave." Heather poured herself a large glass of tap water, found the paper and took it up to her room.

An advert stood alone in a box and took up two columns, so Heather knew it must be prestigious: *Commercial Art Gallery Manager.* Even at the lowest level, the salary, she was sure, was considerably more than Will earned. Okay, he'd have to pay train travel, but he could get a season ticket.

As she read the main responsibilities, she convinced herself that it was the ideal position for him. Things like assessing and selecting artwork couldn't be that hard. Liaising with framers and visiting artists surely would be right up his street. He was so good with people from all parts of society and with different ages. Negotiate sales? Why not? As for promoting and selling artists' work, through both exhibitions and personal contacts, it would be exciting. It was only an extension of him selling his own work, which he did successfully via Cloud 9, the local craft and gift shop. Keeping up to date with industry developments and market trends, well … easy-peasy. A bit of reading, using the library to get information wasn't tricky at all. It really sounded great.

General administration, budgeting, finance and accounts were the only things she wasn't sure about, but hey, that was her thing back in the day, before she came to the care home. She could help him with that.

The ad finished by saying: *Depending on your role, you may focus more on the front of house or behind the scenes.* Perfect. The working hours demanded flexibility. If an exhibition was happening, then the day would be finished when the event was finished. It was clear about that. He worked shifts now, so that should be all right.

Heather was excited at the prospect and bounced down the stairs to tell her mum. "Look at this." She folded the paper back and thrust it in front of her.

June pulled her head back to read. "Sounds very upmarket. What's that all about?" Then she looked up at Heather. "Oh, lass," she said, "you're not thinking of Will, are you?"

"It sounds perfect. He'd be earning so much more. And he'd be on the rungs of a ladder with more kudos, which could really go somewhere. He'd be using his talents and skills."

"I think he's using those where he is now. This new-found confidence of yours... Don't overstep it, love."

Heather was on a roll. Of course she wasn't overstepping it. This would be right up Will's street and with more money, perhaps they might even start flat hunting ... together.

"How are you and Will getting along?" Izzy asked as Heather brushed her hair. "I hope it's all going well. I think you're good for each other. I was so pleased when you got together. He's a lovely chap and works so hard here. Gets on with all of us."

"We had a lovely New Year." Heather told Izzy all about it. "I was thinking of showing him this." She produced the newspaper advert which she had cut out, folded carefully and put in her pocket.

"Oh, I see," Izzy said as she read it. "We'd be sorry to lose him. Is that really what *he* wants?"

"Please don't say anything to anyone. I want to talk to him about it later."

"I won't, dear." A frown passed across her face.

Maybe Heather knew, deep down, that something might not be right, but without thinking deeper about it she sought to deflect any more conversation. "Last time we spoke, Izzy, you told me you were hoping to marry Garrit, and he might come over here to live. Would you tell me what happened?"

"Oh, well, right. Just after I left Berlin that time when we found his mother, the Soviets caused the blockade by closing all rail, road and canal links to West Berlin. They said they'd drop that if the Western allies did away with the new *Deutsche Mark* currency. It was a rare old stand-off. West Berlin was starving to death."

"I've heard of the Berlin Airlift. Was it at that time? Not sure what it was, though," Heather said.

"You have a lovely gentle touch," Izzy said, looking at Heather in the mirror before them.

CHAPTER 31

England, 1950

Izzy received regular letters from Garrit, but with each one she realised he was never going to come and live in England. The last letter had left her depressed and lonely, but she was coming to terms with her long-distance relationship and understood that it was to be an intermittent thing. Her visits to Germany had always been sporadic, and she used those to brighten her otherwise nondescript existence. She read the beginning of this new missive out loud to her papa as they sat either side of the fire on a chilly winter's evening. He had always been forward-thinking, and she enjoyed their chats about politics and world events.

November
Mein Liebling,

She glanced across at Papa, but he gave no sign of any emotion about Garrit's address. He was long past being surprised at the antics of his daughters, she supposed, and continued with a lighter heart.

The times in which we find ourselves are changing so fast. You told me of an airlift of food to the West of Berlin. We have heard next to nothing of this. If the West were not so decadent, we are told, they would have plenty of food. Instead they spend their money on frivolous things. The Western Allies should be doing more for their people in stamping out remaining fascism. Our leaders here in the East are unsure that the West are doing sufficient to de-nazify.

Now, you may have read that our ruling party, which is a unification of the Communist Party of Germany and the Social Democratic Party here in the East, formed the Socialist Unity Party. When we voted for the German People's Congress, we could only vote for candidates from the anti-fascist coalition. Perhaps this is the way to get things done. As a Marxist-Leninist party, the Unity lot have nationalised industrial plants and some infrastructure and I must say we are seeing some benefits here, although we still must queue for things like fruit. Now, since a couple of months ago, we have the new German Democratic Republic. With that, and reparations for the war, we are doing quite well. Seventeen thousand factories from that are helping our economy.

"Reading between the lines, it doesn't sound very democratic to me," Izzy said to her papa, before reading on.

I miss our talks about such things. Mama is not wanting to read much about politics these days. She is so vulnerable and susceptible to depression since her experiences (you understand my meaning) but still takes great interest in several groups that knit things for soldiers and put together tins for the poor.

"Right. That's about it for now. Shall I make us some tea, dear Papa?"

Mr Strong gave her a sideways look and a small smirk played at the corners of his mouth, telling her he knew full well that the next part was for her eyes alone.

Izzy rose with speed, folding the thin notepaper and secreting it in her pocket. She determined to read it all later, when she was alone. It was these words that she had left unspoken that kept her going.

Oh, mein Liebling, I long for the feel of you. I miss our nights together. I hope you can come and visit again soon so I might have you next to me. I remember the last time you lay here with your head on my pillow and we talked of not watching the bridges that we burn. We spoke for hours, didn't we? I know you may find another, but I shall be here whenever you need me.

I cannot leave here when Mama is so vulnerable, and I know you would find it too hard to live here. We are both in the same situation with our parents.

Right now, as I lie here in bed writing this, I hear the whisper of the raindrops against the window and remember that last time we loved. I know we cannot think much about our tomorrows, and certainly not about our forever. The good times we had bear me up and I look forward to the time we can be together, even briefly.

A tear rolled silently down Izzy's cheek and into the corner of her mouth, so she tasted salt. The letter dropped to her lap. She sat as still as the stars that looked down on them both. Surely she would return to his side again soon.

She folded the paper with care and put it in a box with the others.

CHAPTER 32

1956

Izzy had faithfully been back to Berlin for two weeks every year. She had settled into this routine and no one at home seemed to realise that she and Garrit were carrying on their love affair in this way. If they did, nothing was said. She was certain they all saw her as the buttoned-up sister who liked to wear her middle-aged clothes and several layers at that. Her lilac scarf around her neck and her caring for their aged father was her lot. She didn't complain, because for a fortnight each year she had a vibrant and abandoned time in East Berlin, albeit among the grey apartment blocks that were rising all around.

When the East German leaders met Stalin in Moscow in 1952, the Soviet foreign minister, Vyacheslav Molotov recommended a system of passes for visits between the two halves and that the border was not just any border but a dangerous one. Barbed wire fences were erected, although in Berlin things were easier. Stalin died shortly after but Nikita Khrushchev, while repudiating his predecessor's policies in many areas, still crushed the 1953 workers' uprising in a brutal fashion when their quotas were raised by ten per cent and their demands for economic reforms were denied.

In 1954, the Soviet Union gave East Germany sovereignty and the Soviet Control Commission was disbanded, although the Soviet army remained. The United States, Britain and France did not recognise the fifteenth district of this new 'country' that was East Berlin.

There were far more people leaving East Germany than wanting to relocate there, but it was perfectly possible for Izzy to visit, providing she had the correct documentation. There were very few British travel agents who could supply her with what she needed, but she tracked one down in Manchester.

"My dear, why on earth do you want to go there?" The lady she spoke to looked aghast. "All the guidebooks tell us the hotels are scruffy and service is poor. Mind you, most of those books are American so they might be a tad biased." She laughed. "Let me see." She spent a long time perusing several different books, including Fodor's. "Mmm, there's a lot of fortifications now. Thirty-two railway lines, three autobahns closed. There are three air corridors, though."

"I'd rather go by train, if possible," Izzy said. "So much cheaper."

The agent looked her up and down. "Yes, of course. Now, it says here, you must submit your itinerary to the East German state tourist office at least nine weeks before you travel, and you must pay the booking fee. When you arrive…"

"I have to register with the local police. Yes, I know that. I've been before."

"Oh, I see."

"I have friends there."

"Oh!" She said again, with a degree of incredulity. "So, you know you can only stay in the prescribed state-owned hotels."

"Yes, thank you. I have that organised. Here." Izzy handed over a piece of paper with the name of the hotel in question.

"You will have to change trains at the border."

"Yes, East Germany prefer to use their own rolling stock," Izzy said with controlled patience. She knew how slow the journey thereafter would be, that train crews would be changed, sniffer dogs employed for stowaways, though who would do that to get *into* East Germany was beyond her. The train would chug its way slowly on a track that was in poor condition and her passport and visa would be checked and re-checked. With growing animosity between the Soviets and the West, this was all becoming more and more time-consuming.

Still she anticipated her arrival with eager enthusiasm, and it would all be worth it to be in Garrit's arms again. Buttoned-up she might be ... at home. But there, in a foreign land and one that had done much to shape her in those days long past, she was able to show her love with freedom.

Izzy was nearing her destination when she saw a sign for Berlin Grunewald. Had Hannah been sent from Gleiss17 there, to her first concentration camp? It was a former freight track, now with a memorial to those who had been taken and shipped out in cattle trucks.

I wonder what happened to those trucks, she thought. *How can Hannah and other persecuted millions bear to hear the noises of a railway?*

Garrit met her at the final station. He spread his arms wide as she hurried, as best she could with her two bags, along the platform to the barrier. She could hardly believe she was here again at last. After showing her papers yet another time, finally they were together again.

That night they lay in each other's arms, her head on his pillow as they regarded each other and spoke in whispers. She knew complete contentment at that moment. Their loving was pleasure, comfort and fulfilment. The only tiny glitch at the back of Izzy's mind each time she came here was Hannah Shain's attitude towards her. She was perfectly polite, seemed pleased to see her, but Izzy knew that Hannah didn't wholly approve of her good Jewish son cavorting with a *nokri*, a gentile.

"You know *Mutti* does not mind. We speak of this every time you come, *mein Liebling*." He smiled gently and stroked her hair. "She has seen so much horror, she wants us to be happy. Those days of disapproval have long gone."

Izzy was not certain of this but didn't respond. She was determined to put Hannah's old-fashioned opinions from her mind and to relish her time here with her beloved man.

Izzy stroked her finger across Garrit's temple, where grey was smattering the black. When she had looked closely at her own image in the mirror, she saw streaks between her colour too. Older years suited him, though. Her stomach clenched at the thought of him seeing her as a middle-aged spinster. Men were approved, complimented for their looks when the same age or older than she. Her thoughts flitted to Cary Grant, who she had seen in *To Catch a Thief* only recently. Then there was Clark Gable. He was still making a host of films, and although *The King and Four Queens* was a bit corny, he was still renowned for his charm and attractiveness to women of all ages. It wasn't the same for her own sex. Not at all. They were past their prime and unceremoniously dumped when they reached that 'certain' age. What would happen to her? Would Garrit get fed up with her turning up each year?

He must have noticed something in her expression. "What is it? You aren't sorry you came, are you?"

"I'm not. I love you still." She pressed herself against his naked form beneath the sheet. *But I wonder if perhaps you will still like my body, as it is becoming older*, she thought.

CHAPTER 33

Yorkshire, 1976

Will was working late, so Heather waited until she had finished her shift and he would be heading to the little kitchen for his break. In anticipation of talking to him about the exciting job possibility, she half-filled the kettle, switched it on and found two mugs in the cupboard above.

She intended to sit and wait but found she was nervous. The thick white envelope and pile of papers sat in the middle of the table. She leaned against the worktop and took the piece of paper from her pocket and reread the job advert.

As she read, Heather wandered over to the window and then looked down on the garden at the front of the building. The large copper beech trees shaded some grass and a flower bed that had recently been formed into a more secure area by the building of a picket fence. A couple of tables with wooden chairs finished it. Half of the woodwork was painted white. Will must have been doing that today. Some residents were rather forgetful and inclined to wander. At least the fence would stop them roaming onto the road and away.

As she looked down, she spotted Will as he emerged from under the broad canopy of leaves into her line of vision. He carried a large tin of paint in one hand and a brush in the other. His fair hair was ruffled by the breeze and there was a splodge of white on the thigh of his jeans. He looked up and, seeing her, waved the brush in salute as his long legs strode across the grass, and she raised her arm and wiggled her fingers at him. His smile, even from that distance, made her heart beat faster. She took a deep breath, folded the paper and replaced it in her pocket. She then turned to put some Maxwell House coffee powder into each of the mugs and paced the little room.

She was agitated, unsettled. She stepped around the table and rearranged the coffee, tea and sugar containers on the worktop. The muscles in her shoulders were tense. She reread the ad, yet again. *It's great*, she thought. *He would be good at it. No, it's more than that. It's perfect.* She nodded firmly. At the back of her mind was that little sliver of an idea from when she had first seen the advert. It had sneaked its way into her heart. If he earned more and they pooled their resources, could they, would they be able to move somewhere together?

It's only a suggestion, anyway, this job, she thought.

Her eyes slid to the neat pile of paper in the middle of the table, the top one with the logo of the Art Gallery. The details and application form she had sent away for had arrived in a thick envelope this morning.

Heather pulled herself upright. She wasn't nervous, she persuaded herself. She was excited. This would be a marvellous move for Will. She was impatient for him to arrive so that she could share her find with him.

The door opened and she jumped. "I didn't hear you coming," she said and gave a small laugh. "I've made you a coffee."

"Thanks, that's great. I don't have much time. I had to wash the brush, but since you were at the window, I hoped you'd still be here. I was going to ask you…" He came around the table and kissed her lightly as if his mind was somewhere else. *Painting, probably*, she thought and smiled to herself as he sat down.

"Oh? You wanted me?"

"I was going to ask you…" he repeated.

She held up her hand. "Just before you do, I wanted to show you this. It's really exciting." She pushed the sheaf of elegant white paper towards him.

"What's this?" He looked up at her from his seat at the table. He had white paint on his fingers.

"I hope that's dry," she nodded at his hands.

"Yes. It is. Why?" He sounded suspicious.

"Well, you wouldn't want to mark and damage that little lot."

"Heather…" He indicated the smart logo.

"Just read it. Please." Hastily she sat opposite him, tucked her legs under the chair and leaned forwards, her arms resting in front with her fingers linked together so that her whole body was bent towards him.

"What … is … this?" He frowned as he looked her in the eyes.

She hesitated. "It's so great. It's a fab opportunity. You could do it all easily. Look at the salary."

"It's got my name, but it has your address." He had pulled the envelope out from the bottom of the pile of papers. "You sent for this on my behalf?"

Heather nodded vigorously. "It sounds so you. So much better than what you're doing here, now."

"But I have a job which is very … me. This one. Here! And why have it sent to your address? Did mine not sound 'fab' enough?"

Why is he sounding sarcastic? thought Heather. "No, of course that's not the reason." This was all going horribly wrong.

Will spoke dangerously quietly and he looked livid. "Do you not like having a boyfriend who is *only* a caretaker?"

"Don't be ridiculous." She raised her voice.

"Oh, so I'm ridiculous now as well as inferior and…"

"Will!" She interrupted him. "I'm not saying any of that. It's an opportunity, that's all. Look at the money."

"I work here because I like it. I'm doing a good, worthwhile job. I told you that the other night. I have reasons not to work away from home." His finger stabbed the table with each sentence. "We've been through all of this before. I said it again the other night, if you'd been sober enough to listen." His finger pointed at her for this last statement. With that, he slammed his chair back, picked up the sheaf of paper and threw them down. "And if you're ashamed of that, then tough. I'll see you around."

She sat without moving for several moments before leaning down to pick up the papers that had slid across the table and shot onto the floor. Her heart was thudding. Reasons not to work away from home? What did he mean?

Had she misjudged this so very badly? It would seem so. Slowly she stood and picked up the mugs with the untouched drinks, still hardly believing the depth of his anger. As the liquid gurgled down the drain, the bitter smell of coffee rose to greet her.

He had thought she'd meant he wasn't good enough. Her legs were like jelly and she collapsed back into her chair. Her head sank into her hands. How could she have been so stupid, so insensitive? Of course he was good enough. Better than good. He was kind and funny, thoughtful and caring. She loved his family and was comfortable in their home with them. The thought of upsetting anyone, never mind Will, was against her nature, but the thought of losing him altogether was... She suddenly realised that was devastating.

She jumped up, grabbed the papers and stuffed them into the swing bin in the corner. If she was quick, she would find him before he got too involved in his next task. He must understand.

In his shed at the back of the home, there was no sign, nor was he in any of the obvious rooms. He wasn't in the dining room or kitchens. She couldn't find him anywhere. He wouldn't have gone home early, she was sure. He wasn't likely to be doing any outside tasks, but she scouted around anyway.

"Have you seen Will?" she asked Sue on reception.

"He went out the front door about ten minutes ago. Didn't look very happy. In a bit of a rush as well."

"Thanks." Heather went to her locker, retrieved her bag and then hurried out to the front. She looked left and right, but there was no sign of Will. Round the side of the building, her bike was propped against the wall. She stepped towards the thick bushes. "Will, are you there? Will, please, if you're in there, let's talk." She strained to listen.

Was that a rustle of leaves, the crack of a twig? She stood as still as a stone, trying to see past the branches and shiny leaves of the rhododendron bushes. Suddenly she was back to the scared and unadventurous girl who had raised his ire for disturbing the badgers last spring. She dithered about what to do. If he didn't want to speak to her, she would be forced to leave it. She had no torch to go pursuing him in there. One last try. "Will, please, let me explain. I'm really sorry."

Silence.

Agitation bloomed in her chest. It was thick and viscous, sucking away the air until she could barely breathe. She leaned against the wall, unsure what to do and feeling sick. Several minutes passed before, with a heavy tread and a sense of dread, she turned her bicycle and walked up the drive away from the home and away from Will.

CHAPTER 34

Germany, 1961

As she approached the last major obstacle in her arduous journey to East Germany yet again, Izzy was in a daze. She was exhausted. How had things come to this? Her home from home, Germany, in such a state. Well, she had read the news and understood the rhetoric of the Soviets' 'Anti-Fascist Protection Rampart'. It had started years ago with the tensions leading to the Berlin Airlift, and probably before that. Then there was the timber and wire border between East and West, although that could be crossed almost anywhere for years. The so-called 'brain drain' from the Eastern Bloc countries had worried the Soviets during the intervening years. They viewed it as damaging to their political credibility and economic viability.

Berlin became the flashpoint because the border there was easier to cross than anywhere else. This beloved city was a shadow of what it had been in those heady days of her youth. She had been carefree and enjoyed sampling all that it had to offer. She never saw Gisela these days. They had grown so far apart in their views. Izzy didn't even know where she was. She'd probably fled to Argentina or somewhere. Perhaps her husband, the not so delightful Otto, had received a just punishment.

Last year during her visit, Garrit had shared with her the booklet that the East German Soviet Unionist Party had published, where it described the serious nature of people leaving the German Democratic Republic: '...leaving the GDR is an act of political and moral backwardness and depravity'. Later in the piece it said: 'Is it not an act of political depravity when citizens, whether young people, workers, or members of the intelligentsia, leave and betray what our people have created through common labour in our republic to offer themselves to the American or British secret service or work for the West German factory owners, *Junkers* or militarists?'

Izzy had scoffed, "*Junkers*? There is no landed nobility who rely on peasant workers with few rights, not these days."

"Really? What about the factory owners who don't pay their workers enough? What about the great capitalists who make money on the backs of others?" Garrit had asked with an earnest expression.

Izzy would not argue with him. Not when her time was so limited. He would never understand the basic differences in their ideology. Not anymore.

While she was certain that Garrit did not wholly buy into what she considered to be propaganda, over the years his views had been distilled because of all he heard each day. He would not leave. This was his home. She guessed his ailing mother had been the cause originally, but now it was too late. No one was permitted to leave the German Democratic Republic.

Whether the idea originated from Khrushchev or Ulbricht, the GDR State Council Chairman, no one yet seemed certain. When John Kennedy, the President of the USA, had said at the Vienna Summit earlier this year that the USA would not oppose the building of a barrier, it was presented on the news as a grave error. The barbed wire had gone up overnight and the 13th August had become known as 'barbed wire Sunday'. Construction of the wall followed with speed. This was the first time Izzy had seen such a thing. It was terrifying in what it represented.

There was only one border crossing for her, as a foreigner, to use and that was Checkpoint C. The other two were used for transporting goods and official personnel. Ordinary West Germans and West Berliners could not cross at all initially.

She contemplated the suffering of families split apart. How difficult this must be for them, both financially and emotionally. How could they have known it would all be so swift? At least Garrit had his mother with him. They were an island of two, with no other family to lose.

In 1965, she approached the point with complex emotions. Her heart sank again at the sight, but she was still full of anticipation at seeing Garrit again.

The crossing point was built at the junction of *Friedrichstraße*, with *Zimmerstraße* and *Mauerstraße* which, for historic reasons that had nothing to do with the present climate, meant Wall Street. *How prosaic*, Izzy thought.

The Wall was taller than it had been initially and now must be ten or twelve feet high, the top encased by a smooth strip of pipe.

I suppose that's to make scaling it more difficult, Izzy thought with a cold sinking inside. She could see on this Western side, as she approached, graffiti had started appearing along the length.

The car she was in stopped to let her out. She would go through on foot. She shrank as she looked at all the officialdom and at the solid structures ahead of her. Then she straightened her shoulders. As she always had done, with the same spirit that her sister Delphi had, and Rose too, in her quieter way, she would cope with this in her own indomitable fashion.

The wooden hut was in her sight. This is where she would show her papers to the guards, probably American or possibly

British, who would be bored with their posting. They would look at her and see only her middle-aged clothing, her rapidly greying hair pulled back in its bun, and her demeanour. They would think her mad to be going into East Berlin and probably wonder why on earth she, a single older woman, would be doing such a thing, despite the fact she would tell them she was visiting a friend. They would not see the passion inside her soul, or the dramatic life she'd had at times. They wouldn't know the turmoil of her thoughts and the yearning to meet her lover again.

She glanced ahead and to one side. Shadowy figures moved inside the watchtower, so they could see the raked gravel that would indicate footprints, the huge metal Czech hedgehogs to deter and spike vehicles, the death strip, the barbed wire. She could make out the silhouette of the guns they carried at the ready, even from this distance. Her thoughts ran briefly to picture that poor boy, Peter Fechter. Izzy shrank inside. She could only imagine his pain and suffering, shot in the pelvis at eighteen years of age, as he hung on the wire and bled to death in the full sight of the Western guards who dared not venture to rescue him, although they threw him bandages which he could not reach. Screams could be heard for an hour, and no one could believe that he had been so close to getting over the final wall. He wasn't the first to die. Izzy was certain he wouldn't be the last. So many had tried to escape already. Some had managed it. Many had not and paid with their lives.

It might have been tempting to stop at the *Café Adler*, she was so tired. But Izzy was far more eager to see Garrit, who would come to meet her. She looked at the small white hut with its flags for the UK, USA and France with 'Allied Checkpoint C' written above. The notice to her side warned in four languages, 'YOU ARE LEAVING THE AMERICAN SECTOR' in bold black letters.

The physical barrier was different to those first crossings she had made. Since one or two cars had slipped beneath by removing their windscreen and roofs, it was lower and considerably more solid. The footpath was encased in a new wooden fence. Any car must zigzag around the protruding concrete barriers on the road both before and after papers had been checked in the large shed built for the purpose. She could hear and smell the line of them as she walked, lugging her suitcase. All the Volkswagen Beetles and one or two Trabants queued and inched forwards, puffing out their exhaust fumes.

Her silky headscarf slipped forwards and she stopped to push it back from her face, aware that her every movement would be watched. She may even have had a gun trained upon her as she put down her suitcase and paused. She didn't hang around but picked up her case again, changed hands, and with a quick glance back and up, she hastened on.

At last she was through. There was poignancy to this visit, more than any other. In truth, Izzy didn't know how much longer she could do this. She must come to some decisions soon. She scanned her view. The grey buildings and grey people who walked with hunched shoulders looked down at the pavement. In contrast, there was a queue outside a fruit and vegetable shop, but several of the women were laughing together, baskets over their arms as they waited. She put down her suitcase again and pulled the belt of her coat tighter. There was a chill in the air, or was it in her heart?

And then she spotted him. He was hurrying towards her, the tails of his coat flapping with the speed of his stride. His hair was greyer, and as he neared, she saw the crinkles at the corners of his eyes as his smile broadened upon seeing her. He broke into a run, of sorts.

"Izzy, my darling, *mein Liebling*. How I've waited for this moment again."

She accepted his embrace, resting her head on his shoulder, which was so comfortable despite their surroundings. How strange, this love affair. It had lasted for decades, and still she loved him to distraction. Gently he untied her headscarf and stroked her hair, her cheek, ran his thumb across her lips. Nothing more; not in public. It was enough. She knew she was loved.

CHAPTER 35

Yorkshire, 1976

Heather clenched her fingers together in her lap and then looked across at Izzy, who sat hunched in her chair.

"That bit about the wall and the wire, Izzy, that's the stuff of nightmares," Heather said, realising that's where Izzy's dream had originated. "I've heard of it. I vaguely remember something about that young man who died, but I was only about twelve. Mum turned off the TV when it came on the news."

"Yes, desperate people and terrible times. It's ongoing, of course. Not so many people try to escape these days, but still quite a number. Scaling the wall, tunnels, even travelling in a refrigerated truck hidden under meat carcasses. Audacious, yes. Hazardous, absolutely. Reckless, probably. As I say, desperate."

"Did Garrit never try to come here?"

"It's completely impossible. Even since his mother died in 1966, no movement has been allowed."

"But how does he stand it?"

"He's grateful for the work. He still translates. He has a roof over his head and food to eat, albeit repetitive and limited. They are told constantly that they are well off, that economically they are rebuilding still and that the West is depraved and decadent. Even if they are curious about what happens elsewhere in the world, no one will ask or question. Not when every other person is likely to denounce their neighbour to the STASI."

"Who are the STASI?" Heather was bursting with curiosity. "Even though it was difficult, and it must have been very tiring and stressful, did you go back? What about his mum? What happened?"

Izzy sighed, said nothing for a moment and then chuckled. "So many questions."

Heather understood. Izzy needed to change the subject. There was only so much stress she could relive.

"Enough now. Tell me about you," Izzy said. "You look tired, and I've heard on this internal grapevine here that Will is not looking too chuffed with life, either. Have you two had a falling out?"

Over the last couple of days, Heather had thought of little else since the argument with Will. She couldn't concentrate, she was lethargic, her sleep had been broken each night and she'd awoken as crabby as if she'd not had a single wink.

At work, Heather had seen little of Will despite scanning each room she entered. She still couldn't believe how wrong their discussion had gone. At first, she was angry, blaming him for being as arrogant as she first thought. Then reasoning took over, and she was vaguely aware that was unfair. Next, she moved on to excuses. He hadn't listened properly; she hadn't explained clearly enough. Now she was despondent and missing him.

He hadn't changed since she'd first met him. She had. Not only was she missing him, he was missing *from* her. Her heart and mind were telling her she loved him, despite it all. She persuaded herself desperately that his absence from her life was because he was working outside when she was indoors, he was helping his mother with Stella, she'd got his shifts wrong and he'd be in later.

215

Then one lunchtime she entered the dining room and straight away saw his blond head bent towards one of the old gentlemen on the far side of the room. He glanced up as she entered. His eyes pierced her, and she became breathless, but even from this distance they looked angry and dark. She gave a small wave before he looked away without a smile or any sign of recognition. She stood for a second, her hand raised before lowering it, and with haste she glanced around to see if anyone had noticed. As she recoiled, tears came to her eyes, but she looked up at the ceiling and managed to stop them falling. She took her place at a table but if she looked sideways, she could still see him. It was hard not to peek across the room now and again.

"I'm sorry, what did you say?" Heather turned back to the person she was sitting next to.

"I was just saying about my great-granddaughter. She's loving it at school."

"That's marvellous. Such a relief, I imagine." Heather pasted on a smile. It wasn't this old lady's fault that she was in such a pickle.

When lunch was done, Heather had half an hour to herself. She considered searching for Will, but as it turned out she didn't need to go looking. As she left the room, he turned a corner and was ahead of her in the corridor. He must have left the dining room by the other door.

"Will, please, wait."

He turned and stopped walking, but there was no welcoming smile. Heather faltered but walked on until she stood beside him, looking up. His aftershave assailed her nostrils and her tummy flipped.

"Will, I'm so sorry I've upset you." Her heart hammered.

"Do you understand why I'm so unhappy and hurt at what you did?"

She hesitated while she gathered her thoughts.

"No? Well, there we are then. No more to be said." He turned and walked away while she stood and watched his retreat.

She was angry again. *I was only trying to help*, she thought. *He could at least wait to hear what I have to say. I knew he was arrogant. I knew it. I thought it when we first met and now, he's proved it. I've been a fool yet again.*

As she neared the staff toilets, her pace increased until she almost ran through the door. Thankful that no one else was in there, she entered a cubicle and lowering the lid, she sat on it and put her head in her hands. That's when tears came. They were hot and ran down her cheeks and into her mouth. Then her nose began to run. After she dug up her sleeve for a tissue, she blew it vigorously before scrubbing at her eyes. Now she'd have to wash her face and repair her make-up, even though she wore little, and it was all Will's fault. She huffed and took a few deep breaths to calm herself before unlocking the door.

As she soaked one of the green paper towels in cold water and gently pressed it to each eye, she was seething, but the coolness was soothing. Restorations to make-up made, she peered at her reflection. She could see her eyes were still puffy but not as bad as they were. Perhaps she'd get away with it. She flung the main door to the toilets open, still raging, and marched along the corridor towards Izzy's room. It was a happy day when the old lady had arrived as a resident. They got on so well and Izzy was like a granny to her. She never saw her own. Her dad's mother had disappeared as surely as her father, and her mother's mum lived in Spain with some bloke, so she was never around.

Heather tapped on the door, which was already ajar, before pushing it open.

"Hello, dear, come in," Izzy said, turning from the window. "What on earth's the matter with you? You've been crying. Don't deny it. Bring up that chair from by the bed and tell me all about it."

Heather crossed the room and brought over the chair.

"Now, what's the matter?"

Heather fiddled with her fingers and looking down at them, she sighed. Tears threatened to fall again with Izzy's kind tone. She took a deep breath and gave Izzy the gist of it all, including her anger at Will.

Izzy chuckled. "Wind yer neck in, love, as our old Dora used to say. She was a proper Lancashire lass."

Heather gave a dispirited smile at last. "She's the one who looked after you when you were girls, wasn't she?"

"That's right. She was an ordinary working lady, full of warmth and wisdom."

Heather blew her nose again and looked at Izzy, feeling a little better already, though still anxious and wondering what to do. "Maybe if I'd handled it differently, he wouldn't have been so mad at me. Perhaps I shouldn't have sent for the details of the job and let him do that."

"It's no good bargaining now, I'm afraid. What's done is done. Maybe you went at it a bit like the proverbial bull in a china shop."

"Oh, heck. What should I do?"

"Let it rest for a day or two. He won't go gallivanting off with anyone else in that time. He's a serious young man at heart. If he loves you, and I'm guessing he does, he'll be ready to listen to you. After a couple of days, you'll know what to say to him. It sounds like today you didn't have it all straight in your own mind. So when he asked you why he was upset, you weren't sure enough to answer."

"I think I got carried away with my own ideas without thinking of him enough," Heather said.

"More like you've gained confidence but then went over the top. It's not unusual. All your life you've been timid, from what you've told me. Now you're finding yourself and that's a good thing, but perhaps you went too far. We all make mistakes. You'll find your balance. It depends how much you love him. You are the only one to know that. If he's right for you, then you must put up a fight to regain his trust."

"I'm not sure he'll ever want to speak to me again. Perhaps it's easier to cut and run," Heather said.

"Oh, he will, given time. Sometimes the easy, comfortable route is not the best one. I do know about that. You said he came across as arrogant. Well, sometimes that's a sign of low self-worth. He's not as confident as he seems, either. He's had a hard life, with his sister and being the man of the house from a young age. Is he kind to you? Does he boss you around and try to control you?"

Heather shook her head. "No, he's considerate and caring."

"Like I say, if he's the one for you, you must go out of your way to show him that you only want what's best for him, eat some humble pie, put up a fight for him. Show him how much he's appreciated, and he'll climb down off his high horse."

"You're very wise, Izzy."

"I've had a lot of years to learn things. I've made errors along the way, massive ones."

"What do you mean about the easy, comfortable route?"

"Before, you asked me if I did go back to see Garrit. Well, yes, I did. His mother died while I was in England between visits. He was devastated. He had been very self-effacing after he'd found her again, not following his own wishes. He needed to look after her and ensure she was happy. I think he had a lot of guilt because he had escaped to England before war broke out. He'd been over here, perfectly safe, while his parents had experienced untold suffering, the like of which we can only imagine. He never experienced what she did in the camps; the starvation, the workload, the cold or the heat, the lice and dirt and the illness. Death was everywhere. It was almost as if he couldn't forgive himself for not having shared all that. He didn't take the easy route, but I did.

"I'm afraid we had an almighty row the last time I was there because he could have left, before the wall went up, but he didn't. With the benefit of all these years, I believe I could have fought harder to have him. I could have gone to live with him in the East, but I didn't. I was guilty, too, but of taking the easy passage."

Heather sat and looked out of the window at the restless trees as they whipped about in the wind that had grown in strength since she had arrived at the care home that morning.

In silence, she waited to hear more.

CHAPTER 36

East Germany, 1971

Each year, Izzy had crossed into East Berlin at the checkpoint that became known as C for Charlie. Each year, there were a few more defences designed to keep the people in the East from escaping, although they were told it was to keep the Western fascists out.

Now, with these successive moves there were anti-vehicle trenches. These were built to a certain depth and the sides were steep enough to deter tank crossings, never mind ordinary cars. Then there was 'Stalin's carpet', a bed of nails, under each balcony that overhung the death strip between the walls. Barbed wire was a further obstacle, tumbling in great coils across the land.

Watchtowers sprouted up like static triffids, watching and waiting; the titular antagonists of the dictator. Again, barbed wire encircled them at different levels, ugly and threatening.

Everywhere there was a deadly capability, as over ninety people had discovered by the time Izzy was making her tenth visit. As if the death of Peter Fechter hadn't been horrific, harrowing and blood-chilling enough, when Jörg Hartmann was shot at ten years of age as he clung to the wall, there were few Westerners who believed the stories put about by the East that he had been involved in an accident.

For many years Izzy had restrained from being critical of the situation in which Garrit lived. Over the years his perception had changed, and she found herself biting her tongue more and more. It wasn't too surprising, Izzy decided. All the media in the East fed the people with propaganda and she thought they had little or no opportunity to disprove what they were told. Prosperity did increase and there were even some consumer goods to be had, although queues at some shops were just as great. Garrit began to believe that he was better off where he was.

Izzy and Garrit still enjoyed each other's company. He was still caring and attentive. Even though they were in their late middle years, she knew he loved her as tenderly as he always had, and their passion was consummated frequently.

As they lay side by side, her head close to his on the pillow after a particularly satisfying time, his arm came across her stomach and he caressed her naked torso. Before moving to her cheek and hair, he kissed her tenderly. It was innocent conversation that started the argument because, on this occasion, she didn't swallow her words and they popped out unheeded.

"You know, we do have it good here in the East. Our leadership are committed to the advance of scientific knowledge, and I'm getting a lot of work because I speak good Russian as well as German. We have a culture with a healthier and more authentic mentality than West Germany."

"Oh, and how do you know that? Have you been to West Berlin?"

He laughed. "Of course not, and why would I want to? We have our own *Schlager* music culture, good theatre and cabaret. As for our film industry, it's prolific. I went to see a sequel of *The Sons of The Great Mother Bear* the other day. Do you remember we went together to see the original about five years ago?"

"I do. It portrayed the Sioux as the good guys and the American soldiers as the baddies. Inverted the Western cliché good and proper."

"Exactly, and was probably more honest for that."

"It's all state-run, though. You're being drip-fed all the time."

"Sorry?" Garrit withdrew his arm and looked at her, seeming to notice at last that Izzy had been distant while he pontificated. Now, when she spoke, she sounded abrasive, cutting, even to her own ears.

"I'm just saying, it's all what they want you to watch and hear. There's no sharing of cultures or ideas. It's narrow in the extreme, and anyone who offers an alternative view is very frowned upon. They might even get carted away in the night and never be seen again."

"That's ridiculous." Garrit sat up and she regarded his back; the creamy skin she had stroked, the small blemishes she knew so well, the bones of his spine she had fingered as he'd kissed her, the shoulders she had clung to as he'd entered her only minutes earlier.

"It's not ridiculous, Garrit. It's how it is."

"If you would only come here to live with me, you would see." He sounded bitter and resentful. "I know you don't want to. You've made it clear. You don't need to be frightened, but you are." He looked over his shoulder at her. "You can't let yourself do it, can you?"

Izzy was silent, then she sat up and put her arm around him. "We've spoken of this before, but it's impossible. I could no more live here in East Germany than..." Her words ran out, but she had said enough already.

Garrit swung his legs over the side of the bed, and his movement made her arm fall back on the sheet. "Exactly," he said.

As he stood and disappeared into the bathroom without a backward look, Izzy was bereft and very frightened. Her throat thickened and she thought she might vomit. He had never been aloof or glacial like that with her before. Heat rose up her body, under her arms, around her neck, strangling her thoughts.

How could she possibly come to live here with him? Her papa was still living, albeit very frail. Even if he passed away tomorrow, she could not contemplate this life with the STASI watching every move and not knowing who she could trust; people informing on their neighbours; being told what to think and believe by the Soviets.

Then she vacillated. *Although, I suppose, on a day to day basis for ordinary folk that doesn't impinge at all. Not much, anyway. If you get on with life and don't speak out, all is like anywhere else. Almost.* Her thoughts were frantic. Garrit went to work, came home, ate, went to the cinema, went for a walk in the park. How was that so very different to what she did?

If she lived here, though, even if the GDR was recognised as a definitive country, which seemed more and more likely, she wouldn't be able to travel freely back and forth as she did now. How could she give up her family? Even for Garrit, who she still loved, she couldn't contemplate that. How could she say goodbye to all she had known?

While he was in the bathroom, she thrust on her clothes. He returned and did the same in silence. Things had altered subtly between them.

"Coffee?"

She nodded, hardly daring to speak in case her voice broke and tears ran. She pulled a grimace without realising it.

"I'm not offering you a cup of poison. No need to pull that face." He turned away towards the tiny kitchenette on the other side of the room.

The *Robusta* Vietnamese coffee here was not what she was used to. It was the best of what was available, unless you spent a fortune on the depleting resources available from Brazil.

That just proves my point again, she thought. Then her natural feistiness kicked in and she responded in a raised voice. "You have no idea. They tell you what's good and you believe them. Brainwashed."

"Keep your voice down. Do you want the neighbours to think you are a *Frau Fischverkäuferin*?"

"It's not me as a fish seller you fear. It's being reported to the STASI at every turn." She was truly angry now. All the pent-up thoughts came pouring out. "You all spy on each other," she hissed. "It's turning even you into a … a … radical commie."

Love might endure, but bitter words could not be unsaid. She could hardly have voiced anything that would upset him more, and as soon as the words were out, her regret was immense. She flung herself down on the unmade bed and covered her face, her knuckles tightly clenched.

She whispered, "I'm sorry. I didn't mean it. I didn't."

The rest of the week sped by. There was a truce between them, but it was an awkward one. Izzy did all she could to apologise. Although Garrit said he accepted her words, she knew some irreparable damage had been done, and all because she was frightened of the commitment for which he asked, since he no longer had the choice to leave.

The night before her departure, they sat outside with a glass of wine each and Beethoven's *Moonlight Sonata* playing softly in the background.

Garrit raised his glass to her. "To you, my love, and thank you for giving the moonlight something worth shining upon," he said quietly. "When you're gone, I shall look up at it and remember this moment, knowing the same moon radiates on you as well as me. It will connect us. We will always be together, no matter what the future brings. Perhaps there will be something to unify us all one day. I shall think of you walking towards me."

Izzy shifted in her seat and turned to face him. "And how will that be?"

"It will be like … well, you're my moon or indeed my sun. You're a warm breeze. You know, that breeze that stirs when there's a fine rain misting the window. Whatever the weather, the season, your smile will light us both as you come towards me."

She slipped off her chair and knelt at his knee. "I'll pray for that time. A search for the heart is a brave thing, but to find what we have had is the ultimate treasure. I've held it dearly."

Garrit leaned down and kissed her with a rare tenderness. "I've loved you with all my heart, totally, and to the exclusion of all others."

It wasn't until later, when she lay by his side after lovemaking that was sensitive and generous, that she stared into the dark and replayed the scene in the garden. Then she realised the conversation was like a goodbye. They had both spoken as if it was all over for the foreseeable future, acknowledging something that was still not quite definitive but most likely. A single tear rolled down her cheek.

CHAPTER 37

Yorkshire, 1976

Heather leaned forwards, engrossed in Izzy's words. "What happened? You went back to Germany, didn't you? You said you both spoke as if it was over. I can't bear it." Her voice broke on this last sentence.

"The following year, I made all my plans as usual. I had come close to not going, I admit, but when the time came, I couldn't resist it. I couldn't resist him. It was a long-winded process, and I remember I was not looking forward to the tediousness of the journey. I could have flown, but it was so expensive. As it was, it was very tiring and monotonous, and there were so many obstacles, what with stops, changes of trains, and border checks. I had all the permissions, though, and a date was set."

Izzy said nothing for several moments and Heather waited. She watched the old lady, noticing the lines on her cheeks, the tawny spots on her jawline. Her blue eyes, still bright but with a watery film, gazed into the distance, and her lashes, now grey with age, swept down and up again as she sat and looked out of the window. Heather had never contemplated the love of older people much before. Now she knew there was as much passion, desire, intensity and sensitivity as she had in her own life.

She was about to say something to prompt the old lady when Izzy continued. "The week before I was due to leave, Papa died."

227

"Oh, no!"

"It wasn't totally unexpected. He was a great age and had been failing for quite a while. He collapsed in his study one day, and that was it. He died the next day of a massive heart attack. It was still a shock for us all. He was an amazing man in his way, very forward-thinking in his time. After all, he allowed my sister Rose to attend Oxford University in an age when that was remarkable, for a woman. He held us all together when Delphi made her shocking announcement in 1917 and she went off to Australia with her daughter's grandparents. Anyway, of course I couldn't go away when he died. I lost all my bookings and the East German government cancelled my reservations and permissions. There was a lot to do at home, even after the funeral. Delphi wanted to get back to France. Her husband waited there for her. He couldn't leave the vineyard to come over with her. Rose's husband Michael was unwell by that time, too, so she couldn't do much. I had the house to sort out and Papa's papers and affairs."

"What about the following year?"

Izzy gave a small shrug. "I don't know. It all seemed too much. It wasn't going anywhere. My fault, I know. I took the easy passage. Having broken my annual habit, it all seemed so … so … *pointless*. I didn't fight for Garrit hard enough." The old lady turned to Heather. "Which is why you must. If you think Will is the one for you, don't take the easy route. Fight for what you want and be determined. There will be a reason why he works here. Find it. Understand him. Decide what his strengths are and if you like what you find, then fight. I've said this before, but it's so important. Don't live with regrets." She looked away before saying quietly, "They haunt you for a very long time, my dear."

The next few days dragged. Heather found it difficult to smile at the residents. Perhaps this was depression, this lack of awareness of herself and others, this listlessness. She didn't care about anything, and everything was hard work. She cried when alone at the smallest thing, and there was certainly no joy.

Heather's thoughts revolved for days until she understood this could not continue. She decided to find Will on Friday, at the end of the day when she knew he had little else to do that couldn't wait. She went around to the back of the care home. Leaves had fallen and gathered in the corners, blown there by the wind. The outhouse in which Will stored his equipment and hung his coat came into view.

Beside the closed door she took a deep breath and then knocked with determination, before opening it and entering. It was warm inside after the stiff breeze that had ruffled her hair. The huge old-fashioned cast-iron stove within its tall black guard stood opposite the door, dominating the space. Will was nowhere to be seen, but his coat still hung on the rack to her right.

Heather huffed. Since she had built herself up to this, she was deflated to find him absent. She took a couple of paces forwards and stood by the long trestle table, marvelling at how busy he must be. There were spanners and a hammer lined up at one end; a can of WD-40; a paint tray and some brushes; a dustpan with a small pile of sawdust waiting to be disposed of; and a notebook.

The last item was closed, but Heather was tempted to peep inside. She ran her index finger under the card cover and raised it a couple of inches. The first few pages, as she turned them with her thumb, were dated and jobs were listed. It was highly organised, with notes on how long each job took to complete.

The next page made her remove her finger with haste and step back.

Her own image had looked back at her and she had read a title: *Heather Honey, my lost love in a wilderness.* It was dated yesterday. Only yesterday? After looking over her shoulder, she peeked again at the sketch. There were notes haloing the hair of the figure, relating to colours, background moorland, sky tones, and underneath was a list of pigments. The eyes of her own face looked back at her with intensity, bewilderment. Lost? These last few weeks she had been lost. He had remembered and used the nickname her father had given her. Suddenly it took on a whole different meaning.

So intent had she been, looking at herself through his eyes, she didn't hear footsteps approaching. She was hardly aware of the door opening. A breeze wafted past her, and she turned to see Will standing in the doorway. She gasped. The setting sun behind him was bright, and she couldn't see his expression. Would he be further annoyed with her for prying? She put her hand to her chest.

He turned and closed the door before advancing slowly across the room, regarding her face the whole time. She clasped the table behind her with one hand.

"Will, I…"

His hand came to her face and his thumb lightly skimmed her left eye and then her right. She realised he was wiping her tears.

"Will, I'm so, so sorry." She looked at his shoes, vaguely noticing the dust. "I got carried away. I wasn't thinking of you, of what you wanted or why you work here. I've thought about it, and it's obvious. You support your mum. You help with Stella. Working away would compromise that. You are loyal and trustworthy, a family man. I've been a selfish fool. I…" A series of sobs escaped until she was crying with gulping hiccups and tears were streaming down her cheeks.

"Hush, now." His arms encircled her shoulders. "Don't cry, Heather. Yes, you're right. That's exactly why I stay. That and … I like it here. It's a worthwhile job. I'm needed."

"I need you. I…" She gave a hiccup. "I became bossy and heedless." Another gulp. "All the things I detest." Her shoulder heaved again as she wept.

"Shh! I know. And I'm sorry, too. I was thoughtless and didn't see your actions for what they were. You meant well. We've both been foolish." Then he whispered into her hair, "I've missed you." His arms tightened around her, and then he let go and knelt down in front of her. "I have something to ask you."

Later that day, Heather held out her left hand for Izzy to inspect her new engagement ring. "It might be small, but to me it represents so much," she said, feeling self-conscious. "I imagine each of the little diamonds on either side are Will and me, and the centre stone is the family we shall have together."

Izzy smiled.

"I know, I know, it's fanciful." Heather laughed at herself and lifted her shoulders.

"Nothing wrong with dreaming. I'm very, very happy for you, my dear child."

Heather experienced a warm glow. "Can I ask? Are you sorry not to have had a family?"

The old lady chortled. "I have you." Then, after a pause, she added, "I am sorry not to have seen Garrit one last time. We still write and send cards but… Oh well, that's life. I'm certainly too old now, and he can't come here with this blasted situation, the Wall and everything."

"Maybe, one day…" Heather said.

CHAPTER 38

England, 1989

Heather sat on the sofa, kicked off one slipper and tucked her leg under her to watch the news, while Will sat in a chair flicking through the *Radio Times*.

"I wonder if all those images of Tiananmen Square in the spring had any influence on this? I mean, it didn't have the desired effect in China, but Eastern Europe's had all sorts of unrest."

"It has," Will answered as he continued to look at the magazine.

"Do you remember when we watched that *Panorama* programme with that bloke reporting from Czechoslovakia? Gavin What's-His-Name."

"Hewitt."

"Oh yes, well, after that there was unrest in Poland for months and Solidarity won that free election. Hungary started taking down their bit of the Iron Curtain. Wouldn't it be amazing if East Germany had a rebellion?"

"Well, yes, I suppose so."

"Izzy could see Garrit again."

"Maybe, but they're both totally ancient now. Nothing much on tonight," Will said, tossing the magazine to one side. "We've got that Michael Palin thing recorded. We could watch that later. *Around the World in Eighty Days*."

"Oh yeah, I like that. I must just iron a school shirt for Iris before that."

"Do you want me to do it? Or shall I do the packed lunch?"

"It'd be great if you do the shirt, then we can sit down. Maybe a glass of wine. There's a bottle of that nice New Zealand in the fridge. Do you remember when pretty much all we had was Blue Nun?" She laughed and stood up.

Will took her by the shoulders and planted a kiss in her hair before releasing her and going upstairs to the spare bedroom and the iron. "I'll take a peek at the girls and make sure they're asleep while I'm up there," he said.

Heather thought, yet again, how lucky she was to have this gorgeous man for her husband. If it hadn't been for Miss Iris Strong, Izzy, they might never have got it together and she wouldn't have their two marvellous little girls, Iris and Estella. How wonderful it would be if she could do something truly miraculous for her friend, who was so very old now.

Later that week, Heather read to Izzy from a magazine she had sent away for.

"The mass exodus of East Germans into Hungary became more and more dramatic, with people battering their way across the border and running. This began to destabilise the German Democratic Republic. It wasn't long before non-violent demonstrations began. Leipzig held theirs on Mondays starting with a few hundred people and swelling to over seventy thousand and other towns followed on different days, demanding, among other things, freedom of travel. Similarly, a sit-in at the embassy in Prague, Czechoslovakia, for people desperate to cross a border but without relevant documentation became a humanitarian crisis. Many were crammed into the building, where it was hot and dangerously short of sanitation and food. The leaders in Bonn and GDR finally came to an agreement and the reaction to freedom of travel was, not surprisingly, intense.

"Although some demonstrators were arrested, the threat of intervention by security forces never materialised. Local leaders, without clear orders from East Berlin and surprised by the unexpectedly high number of citizens, turned away from causing a possible massacre. They ordered the retreat of their forces.

"The next week, in Leipzig on 16 October 1989, 120,000 demonstrators turned up, with military units again being held on standby in the vicinity.

"Erich Honecker, the leader of the SED, has been forced to resign.

"This week, the number has more than doubled to 320,000."

Heather lowered the magazine. "Oh, Izzy, it's happening, it's really happening."

"I do believe it is." The old lady shook her head. "I can hardly comprehend it. After all this time." She sat slumped in a chair that dwarfed her slight frame. Heather remembered the time she had first come upon her, when she had been having the nightmare about the wire and how she had been brushing and picking at her clothing. Heather now understood why that was. The Wall, the watchtowers and the barbed wire had left their mark. Was the horror of that time really coming to an end?

On the evening of November 9th, 1989, Heather and Will were seated next to each other on the sofa. Heather grasped Will's hand as they sat glued to the television. The images they watched were history in the making. A few tentative young men were first onto the wall, but when nothing happened, hundreds, then thousands followed. A line of Trabant cars queued at Checkpoint Charlie to cross into West Berlin.

A woman from the East was interviewed and said, "It's a miracle." Tears ran down her cheeks.

Someone else made a comment about the myriad colours that assaulted her senses. "It's all so grey over there." She tossed her head behind her. "Here, it's incredible. It's all so bright."

There were images of people chipping at the Wall for a souvenir, with anything from pieces of rock to pickaxes. The crowd was immense on both sides, some drinking from bottles with foam spouting everywhere, many crying and hugging relatives from whom they had been separated for thirty years or more and others hugging complete strangers, but everyone celebrating.

Someone waved a flag with '*Öffnung der DDR Grenzen*' scrawled in spray-paint across its centre. A newscaster explained that it meant opening of the German Democratic Republic borders. He said an announcement was supposed to have been made surreptitiously at four o'clock in the morning, but then at the press conference it was announced that the border was open from that moment and everyone who was able had rushed to the Wall by any means possible.

"Do you think we might manage to bring Garrit over?" Heather asked.

Will looked at her. His expression was sad. "Honestly, Heather, I think that might be a step too far. He's very elderly and probably frail."

She sighed.

EPILOGUE

England, 1990

Almost a year later to that day, at the airport, Izzy sat in a wheelchair between Heather and Will, who were standing beside her behind the tape that separated them from the passengers arriving through the gate. Izzy could have walked, but it would have taken a long time and tired her. The elderly lady glanced up and raising her arm, she took hold of Heather's hand. It was strong and firm compared with her own, which was bony and slight. Her young friend looked down and smiled, excitement lighting her eyes. Izzy's emotions were bubbling, and she was confused by them, but elation was surfacing.

It was nearly twenty years since she and Garrit had said goodbye. He might have changed. Well, surely he would have. She certainly had. She was old, shrivelled, grey and lined. Her chest had sunk, and her shoulders were rounded. She needed a stick to help her to balance as she walked, and she tired so easily. Sleep was her companion most days, although she made sure she took a turn around the gardens when the weather permitted.

Oh, this was a bad idea. What if all her dreams and memories were about to be destroyed? One should never attempt to go back in time. What if she didn't like him? He may well not like her, and he had come all this way. How unfair for him that would be. Perhaps he could visit somewhere interesting or take a drive into the countryside, then return home without too much lost. Why had she been talked into this?

"I think I'll stand now," she said to Will.

He bent to help her to her feet. Oh, he was a lovely boy. So strong and capable and that smile … enough to gladden anyone's heart. *I'm so pleased these two are together*, she thought. *My favourite family. I'm truly blessed that they invite me to their house so regularly and I can enjoy the two little girls as well. Closer than my very own flesh and blood, they've been. How lucky I am.*

Heather and Will came together, his arm around her. She leaned into him and rested her head on his shoulder, taking his other hand in her own. They still liked to touch each other, Izzy noted with satisfaction.

At that moment an elderly man came around the corner, walking slowly with a shuffling gait, barely lifting his feet, with a stick in one hand and his arm linked through that of a woman with dark hair, who looked about half his age. She must be his cousin's daughter.

Izzy's heart skipped a beat. She would know him anywhere, despite the grey hair and slight stooping shuffle.

Garrit. In her eyes, he was dark-haired with just an attractive smattering of grey at his temples. At that moment, he was upright and as handsome as ever, with his brown eyes and ready smile for her alone.

He came towards Izzy. He unlinked his arm and put both out to her. Everyone else disappeared.

They were young again.

A NOTE TO THE READER

Dear Reader,

Thank you so much for choosing this book. Tackling the story of the youngest of the three Strong sisters and including another turbulent time of the twentieth century was a challenge because of the time frame, related to the previous two books, *Sisters At War* and *Resistance of Love*. Then I came up with the idea of reflecting Izzy's tale, as she tells it when elderly, in that of her care assistant, Heather, to write a dual timeline novel.

Although this is not her story, I had great inspiration from a particular relative. When I was a very young child I had a great-aunt who was then in her eighties. Other relations used phrases that were probably more acceptable then and said she was 'buttoned up' and a 'typical spinster'. I remember she used to wear high-buttoned blouses, at least two cardigans with her tweed skirt, and always a lilac woolly scarf. She visited Germany once each year, passing through the Berlin wall at Checkpoint C for Charlie, the place for visitors, and citizens who were not going for business purposes. There was always a bit of a mystery. It wasn't until she passed away, that in her effects, an explanation was discovered. She had been visiting a lover — just for two weeks for years, across many decades. She wasn't so constrained after all, but it was very sad.

I'm particularly fond of this book and really loved writing the story of Izzy with Garrit, and Heather with Will. If you enjoyed reading *The Divided Heart*, you might consider writing a short review on **Amazon** or **Goodreads**. These, from knowledgeable people, are so important for authors' success but also contribute to other readers' choice of a book. If you would like to know more about my writing, my website is **www.rosrendleauthor.co.uk**. You can also **sign up for my newsletter**. I often give free gifts and there is early access and information about my books. I love to hear from readers, and you are able to connect with me through **Facebook** or via **Twitter**. I hope we'll meet again in the pages of my other novels.

Ros Rendle

Sapere Books is an exciting new publisher of brilliant fiction and popular history.

To find out more about our latest releases and our monthly bargain books visit our website:
saperebooks.com